DEATH ON THE
ARKHAM EXPRESS

BYRON CRAFT

DEATH ON THE ARKHAM EXPRESS

Ride the rails with this Cthulhu Mythos mystery!

The Arkham Detective is back! A well-earned first-class ticket on the train from New York to Arkham, intended as a pleasurable trip, is sidetracked into a grotesque journey. Commuters' heads are bashed in by an invisible assailant and the only law on board is . . . You guessed it; our detective from Arkham.

* * *

"Byron Craft goes places HPL never dared."
F. Paul Wilson - Author of THE KEEP, THE GOD GENE, REPAIRMAN JACK SERIES, and much more.
www.repairmanjack.com

"Bryon Craft again takes the most beloved elements of the Lovecraft canon and makes them his own. The fact that he does this while keeping everything readers love about Lovecraft's creations in the first place is astounding."
Sean Hoade - Author of 18 books and pulp writer extraordinaire

"Byron Craft returns to the Lovecraftian with 'Death on the Arkham Express.' Craft's inimitable ability to pay homage to yet make the world of Lovecraft his own is proof positive of his abilities as a writer."
Paul Atreides, www.paul-atreides.com

"Bryon Craft writes cinematic, action-packed science fiction horror with panache: smart plotting, engaging characters and attention to detail put him a cut above the field. If you like your aliens slavering and carnivorous, your heroes rugged and your action explosive, you're going to love his work."

David Hambling, author of the Harry Stubbs series.
www.facebook.com/ShadowsFromNorwood/

"Byron Craft is a master of combining Pulp Adventure with Lovecraftian horrors. When Byron puts pen to paper, he builds a perfect adventure around a core of sheer terror that makes for an excellent read."

Matthew Davenport, author of the Andrew Doran series,
www.davenportwrites.com

DEATH ON THE ARKHAM EXPRESS
Book 5 in The Arkham Detective Series

This is a work of fiction. Names, characters, places and incidents are the product of the author's imagination. Any resemblance to actual persons, living or dead, events or locales is entirely coincidental.

www.ByronCraftBooks.com

Cover art by Marko Serafimovic; Upwork®

ISBN: 9781099792793
Independently published

DEDICATION

To my wife, Marcia, who says she loves me because she lets me watch my crappy TV shows.

Special thanks to my great network of long distance friends that connect, encourage and support my efforts through the great venue of social media.

Also a call out for my daughter and son-in-law who are in the publishing business and keep me thinking outside of the box when it comes to marketing what I've written. The author in me wants to just write, my support group says "spread the word!"

DEATH ON THE ARKHAM EXPRESS

BY

BYRON CRAFT

BYRON CRAFT

DEATH ON THE ARKHAM EXPRESS

Getting a suspect to fess up can be difficult, decidedly difficult when there's five of them especially if one of the mugs ain't human.

That was the double-barreled dilemma I faced when I boarded the train in New York bound for home, Arkham. It was gonna be a leisurely trip for me — a short, but well-deserved vacation. I think the Chief at our Station House knew as much when he sent me on an assignment any rookie uniform could handle with half his brain tied behind his back. Extradite a Lobo in handcuffs to the Manhattan constabulary, where he was wanted for armed robbery, and beat it back the way I came.

I had just come off a case that had me working night and day coupled with a grueling trip to Dunwich. My partner and I nailed the perp we were after while rescuing a Federal agent that had been imprisoned by the suspect. I was dog tired when we got back. A nice size nest egg had dropped into my lap in the interim, and I had been shooting my mouth off about a possible early retirement. I think that's why my boss played Mister Nice Guy and launched me on my cushy duty to the Big Apple. Butter up the old detective in hopes he'll stick around for a few more years.

The job was a piece of cake. Until my waiter, in the dining car, had his head ripped off.

The cuisine on the Arkham Express was limited. They did, however, have a reputation for serving an outstanding hot corned beef sandwich. My mouth watered anticipating my waiter's return. The only thing that could improve the expected meal would have been beer — a couple of ice-cold beers. Unfortunately, I was unable to locate any to smuggle on board. The Feds were still enforcing the Volstead Act, and I didn't know any bootleggers in New York. The word is that next January beer and light wine would become legal. Fat chance. I'm hopin' that Roosevelt will repeal the damn temperance law.

It was taking the young man that took my order a very long time to bring me my dinner. My navel was scratching my backbone. Out of boredom, I was etching little tic-tac-toe emblems with the edge of my fork into the white linen tablecloth. I looked up from my engravings noticing that several of the clientele in the dining car were also growing impatient. All the tables in the restaurant on rails seat four lining the long walls. I sat alone. I tossed my Fedora onto an empty chair. That was when I heard the scream.

In my business, you hear a lot of screaming. Dames can let loose with a piercing holler when the right moment presents itself — faced with impending death at knifepoint or, as typical in Arkham, some hideous nightmare. There was this one filly pushed out a ten-story window. I was standing on the pavement below at the time. Her screams increased in volume as she plummeted closer. Locomotives do that as they exit a tunnel towards you. She was a mess when she hit bottom. Blood, brain matter and long blonde hair splattered the concrete and my slacks. She had been a snappy dresser — light gray wool suit with patent leather purse and shoes. We never found out who or why she was thrown out the window. The Arkham Advertiser reported it as a suicide. I knew better.

This time the long, loud, piercing cry we all witnessed expressed emotion of morbid fear and extreme pain. The crashing of broken dishes and the voices of several women shrieking followed.

I drew my Colt from my shoulder holster with my right hand and produced my badge with my left. "Police!" I shouted. I normally announce "Arkham Constabulary" when the need arises, but I was out of my jurisdiction and keeping things simple had always been my forte. I ran toward the kitchen where the racket emanated.

Blood contains iron, and the metallic smell was extremely strong when I entered. The red painted cookery reeked of the odor. A crimson body fluid spray marred the narrow galley layout of high gloss white walls. Staring at me was my waiter. His head lay grotesquely upon a stainless-steel counter. The features were twisted and torn and mangled. His dead black eyes conveyed a combination of terror and revulsion. It reminded me of the eyes of a dead fish snatched from its peaceful watery existence and decapitated by a hungry fisherman. I didn't wax poetically at that moment because I was glad that I hadn't had my evening meal yet. If I had, I probably would have decorated the kitchen deck with my innards.

Unlike the severed fish, the dining car attendant's head had been ripped from his torso. The two carotid arteries hung loosely leaving bloody trails on the shiny steel already starting to turn brown. A splintered portion of the spinal cord tipped the head sideways. His mouth was wide open as if he was trying to say something.

The headless body of the young man that took my dinner order was stretched upon his back in the center of the galley. Red streaks crisscrossed his white server's jacket and trousers as if put there by some mad impressionist. In the waiter's left hand was a meat cleaver. A peculiar bluish pus or ichor covered both of his hands and the cleaver. Two middle-aged women, I assumed they were the cooks, were frozen in terror at the sight. The galley door on double acting hinges suddenly swung open, and the busboy entered. "Good God in heaven, what happened?" exclaimed the youngster no more than twelve years of age.

"What's your name, kid?" I demanded still displaying my gun and badge.

"Alvin Nash, sir," he replied shaking like a leaf.

"Alvin, take these ladies into the dining car. Under no circumstances are they to leave until I get the opportunity to question them. Tell your customers that the restaurant is closed due to a kitchen malfunction and return to their compartments or seats. But get all their names first, I'll want to question them later."

"Yes, sir," he answered still visibly shaken.

He took the two ladies by their hands and gently led them to the door. He stopped when I hollered, "Hey kid! You stick around as well." He slowly nodded and exited the room.

I had observed something else in the cookery, and I didn't want anybody disturbing the evidence. A straight diet of a horrifying experience was not a good thing for the lady chefs as well, and it was best that I got them out of the kitchen. Next to the bloody torso were footprints. Someone had tracked barefoot through the blood and headed away from the dining area toward the rear door to the adjoining car. The blood-stained tracks were large with oversized toes, probably a man's or either a woman with exceptionally big feet. I followed them.

Toilet facilities are at the end of each carriage before crossing over to a connecting Pullman Car. The footprints disappeared behind the lavatory door. The crazy thing was, as I trailed the unknown assailant, the footmarks gradually reduced in size. Smaller and smaller until they no longer resembled prints made

4

by a human. Footprints of a huge hound? A cold wave of apprehension passed over me. I pocketed my badge and chambered a round in my 1911 Colt. The door to the john was hinged to swing in. I gave it a swift kick and squatted into a two-handed aiming position. It was empty. Six toilet stalls lined a wall and I, in turn, kicked each open in rapid succession aiming the barrel of my .45 straight ahead. Nothing; the damn john was deserted. Little blood spots littered the tiled floor as if made by a small dog. Considering the amount of blood produced by the murder of the waiter a restroom would be the place of choice to wash away the incriminating evidence. I left the lavatory and walked across the platform between the two cars. The chugging, puffing and clickety-clackety sounds of the train traveling the rails was louder on the open-platform. The clickety-clack you hear when traveling by train is due to metal fish plates that join rails; when the train passes over them, you hear those sounds. It is continuous because fish plates are present at intervals of distance dictated by the length of rails.

I didn't enter the Pullman and just peered through the door's window into its interior. It was filled to about half capacity. One fella was smoking a big stogie; two others read newspapers, a third looked furtively around then poured some booze from a hipflask into a coffee cup. Several well-dressed ladies sat on cushioned seats knitting, chatting and reading. One in a blue silk get-up and matching hat read a book that was surprisingly the same color as her outfit. I could faintly make out the author's name on the cover; Emily Brontë. All looked very calm and peaceful. Even if our suspect was able to wash up before entering the next passenger car his clothes would be covered in so much blood that he'd attract a helluva lot of attention. Unless he committed the dastardly deed stark naked and, of course, that would have created a tremendous uproar, a head turner, when entering the Pullman. From where I stood there was no other way he could have gone. Unless he jumped from the train; a speeding train? The drop would surely kill him. The route we were traveling, at that moment, took us along the edge of a steep mountainous ridge overlooking the coast. I returned to the dining car's galley.

I tightened the muscles in my gut and closely examined the detached head of the young man that waited my table. There was a hole in the left temple. I wished I had a magnifying glass like Sherlock Holmes. I pushed my bifocals up onto the bridge of my nose and leaned in for a closer look. The hole was smaller than the end of a pencil. A small caliber bullet? I didn't seem likely. In the close narrow quarters of the galley, there should have been traces of powder burns, there wasn't. Even so, there was only one way to settle the issue. I screwed up my courage and did the next disgusting thing. I grabbed a handful of hair and turned the guy's noodle onto its left side. There was no exit wound on the right.

***

The Arkham Express was a laugh. It ain't no 20th Century Limited. Our little railroad is part of the branch line from Rowley. When the bottom dropped out of the economy in 1929, it didn't go easy on the railroads, and the Rowley Line fell into receivership. The Streamliner Era of transportation passed us by in a few short years. These newer super trains could reach speeds up to 100 miles per hour and carried water tenders that eliminated the numerous stops to refill its boiler. Streamliners, like all locomotives, consume large quantities of water compared to the quantity of fuel, so water tender cars are necessary to keep them running over long distances. These modern monarchs of steel in the third decade of the Twentieth Century speed along the humming rails. Their screaming whistles urging you to "go somewhere."

In contrast, the Rowley Line doesn't have two nickels to rub together so, consequently, they were unable to keep up with the new era. The old locomotives they keep in service chug along the coastal route straining to reach speeds of fifty miles per hour. Not hauling any water tender cars either, meant we had to stop every fifteen miles or so, at station houses, to refill the boiler. We would, naturally, take on additional passengers, freight and fuel at all the major stops on the way, such as Pennsylvania Station and the Providence Station, with, however, the numerous watering holes in between. Consequently, what should be a five-and-one-half hour trip in a more modern coach took us ten. That was why the Arkham Express was such a laugh. We would halt at every whistle-stop. At least the Chief was good-hearted enough to book me a first-class passage.

Winter was around the corner, and it was colder than a witch's upper torso outside. The warmer coastal temperatures mixed with the chilled evening air and thick vapors swirled and eddied causing our train to travel through a blind fog. I'd been standing there contemplating the outdoors and my next move smoking a Lucky Strike. The windows of the dining car presented an imperfect view. There was no other law on board the "Express" and at that moment I decided they should change its name to the "Limited." My limitations were numerous. I'd have to make the best of it until I could drop the murder case into the lap of the authorities at one of the major stopovers. I would normally have my partner, Matthew Bell, do a lot of the preliminary questioning taking all the notes, but he was back in Arkham at Station House 13.

Arkham is a land located in northeast Massachusetts, and at

that minute it might as well be a million miles away. I would have to go it alone. I ground out the Lucky in an ashtray and removed a small pad of paper from my trench coat and a pencil from my shirt pocket. Some guys like to use a fountain pen, but they can mess up a shirt in a heartbeat. When the lead wears down, I whittle it sharp with my knife.

The busboy had done as directed. I counted heads and everyone that was in the dining car when all hell broke loose were present. I started with the two dames that did all the cooking. "What's your name, ma'am?' I asked the one on the left fiddling with her apron strings. Her eyes were red from crying, and her make-up had run.

"Sarah, Sarah Walker, sir," she answered fidgeting incessantly.

"And you?" I said pointing my pencil at the other.

"Ann Hoade, Officer."

"Let's get down to brass tacks, ladies. Tell me what you saw back there in the kitchen?"

"The same as you, Detective. Poor Mr. Wheatcroft's mangled body."

"Who?"

"Donny, Inspector," Alvin Nash, the busboy, interrupted. "Donald Wheatcroft is the rail line dining steward," he added noticing the puzzled expression on my puss.

I wrote Wheatcroft's name down, then nodded and turned back to the lady chefs. "Who did you see in there besides 'poor' Mr. Wheatcroft?"

"No one, sir," they replied in unison.

That flummoxed me. "Weren't you in the kitchen when the . . . murder was committed?"

"No, Officer. We must have been in the washroom at the end of the car changing into our uniforms when . . . it happened," volunteered Chef Sarah.

"We were preparing to come on to the dinner shift," Chef Ann supplemented.

"So, you came in the back way?" They both nodded. "And you didn't see anyone else?" I challenged. I guess I raised my voice a bit too loud because they both jumped.

Chef Ann gathered up her courage and countered with an exasperated air, "Not until you came barging in waving that gun or yours."

The dame had chutzpah. I smiled, "No one else?"

"No one, except later, when Alvin came in," braved Sarah feeding off Ann's pluck.

"And I suppose you didn't see anyone either?" I questioned turning to Alvin 'the busboy' Nash.

"Yes, your honor, not a soul." The kid had done a good job rounding up the usual suspects, but he was also a smart aleck.

It was a big fat dead end. The guy that committed the gruesome murder had done one helluva disappearing act. The dining car patrons proved to be equally useless. They, of course, knew less than I did. I suspected as much all along. They had been witnesses to the blood-curdling screams, never seeing the interior of the galley and never observing anybody coming or going. I yearned for the boys from forensics or a good morgue chemist to do an autopsy. I needed some clues. Right then and there I was clueless.

***

Two of the porters on board had the disgusting job of removing Donald Wheatcroft's head and torso from the galley. Coffins were in short supply, so a waterproof canvas mail sack served as a body bag. I had them put the remains in the refrigerator car. The reefer was located six cars back, and Wheatcroft was bunked down between the cumquats and radishes. It's not a good idea, normally, to monkey with evidence but if we didn't get the corpse out of the kitchen soon, it would stink up the joint. One of the porters, Jenkins, suggested the refrigeration and I jumped on the idea. Putting him in cold storage would preserve the remains until a coroner could have a look see.

Alvin located a couple of lengths of rope for me, and we tied them across the front and back doors to the galley. He also made me two signs out of pasteboard which read, "DO NOT ENTER BY ORDER OF POLICE." I hung them on the ropes.

At the rate we were traveling it would be a while before we reached our first major stop and a big city police department. That left me time to do some snooping. It's best to question witnesses when their memories are still fresh, even if they don't know they are witnesses.

***

"Can I have a few words with you, ma'am?" The lady in blue silk was still in the Pullman looking relaxed and cozy reading her book. There was something familiar about that shade of blue.

"What for?" she answered suspiciously, becoming tense. Her voice was husky, not sultry though. The vocal sound you might hear coming from a hardheaded dame.

"Small talk," I flashed my badge.

"Why should I speak to you?" she answered slapping the book shut with her long dainty fingers.

"Why not? Everyone's been speaking to me. How long

have you been in the Pullman?"

"Ever since we left the station."

"During that time did you see anybody suspicious?"

"What do you mean?" getting defensive.

I leaned closer and lowered my voice. "A short while ago a terrible and unspeakable deed was done in the dining car, and I am trying to corral all the suspects." I thought by appearing to take her into my confidence that she'd loosen up. It had the opposite effect.

"I'm a suspect, am I?"

"No, ma'am."

"Why should I trust you, Mister? Anybody can carry a badge around."

"Just when I was beginning to like you."

"News travels fast on this train. I heard that someone was murdered. I have never left this seat since the train started moving, now leave me alone, or I'll call for the conductor."

The dame was quick to get on her high horse. She panicked easily. "I'm not accusing you of anything ma'am. I just want to know if you saw anybody come through here from the dining car in the past hour?"

"If I say 'no' that makes me a murder suspect. If I say 'yes,' what does that make me?"

"Human, maybe. What are you trying to do, play the bright, hard lady? Are you afraid of life Miss and people? Give yourself a chance and assist with my investigation."

The lady in blue looked down at her lap, opened her book and started to read. Her lips moved silently. I was getting the cold shoulder. I decided to try an even softer approach. "Wuthering Heights," I offered noticing the title on the cover. "You a fan of Emily Brontë?"

"She cocked her head back and glared at me with daggers in

her eyes, "Yes, she's my favorite author. I've read all of her novels."

"Thank you," I said. This time there was sarcasm dripping from my voice. "If it won't disturb you, I will have a talk with this gentleman over here," pointing to the man with the big cigar.

"Do what you like. Don't let him sit there in the cold all chewed up with curiosity."

"I'll break it to him gently." I wasn't good at these parlor room mysteries. Get all the suspects in one place and at the right dramatic moment aim with my outstretched rifle barrel arm proclaiming, "and the murderer is . . ." Not happening. Cigar man was looking in my direction smiling. He was tall, slim with a slight stoop and abnormally broad shoulders. The expression on his face told me that he overheard my conversation with Lady Blue.

"How's it going, pal?" I asked with my partially deflated ego.

He kept smiling. "I am truly sorry. I did not mean to eavesdrop."

"Think nothing of it. Since you have a clue what I'm snooping around for, did you see anyone come through here in the last hour?"

"Possibly. Can we talk in my private compartment?"

"Lead the way."

***

My new best friend stabbed his smoldering cigar into the Pullman's sand ashtray, and we departed for the first-class car. Blue-ribbon passage on the Arkham Express, before time and neglect took its toll, was once a joy to behold, luxurious and fashionable. Nowadays pealed and patched wallpaper lined the hallway walls partnering with threadbare carpeting that guided you to the private compartments. Despite years of impairment the hand carved woodwork maintained its elegant style. Although dust laden, its glossy varnished surface managed to shine through, revealing intricate scroll work. A harmonious arrangement of relief sculptures of animals in foliage in a spiral form crowning the ceiling wrapped in snakes, winged things, and gargoyles peering down on all that walked the hall. The extent of color amongst the different species of dark brown wood used in the sculptures were of such minute detail and mechanical accuracy that if one stared at them long enough the figures appeared to come alive and move. The effect had me in its grasp when I walked along the hallway.

His was the third compartment. Inside, he slid the door closed and drew the curtains. "What I need to say to you requires privacy," taking a seat next to the window, his back to the movement of the train. "My name is Nigel Guest and what do I call you, sir?"

"Detective."

His compartment was a sleeper. Soft purple well-worn cushioned seats, dark mahogany woodwork, with an overhead for luggage at one end, a pulldown bunk at the other, and a large window in between to view the passing scenery. "Your compartment appears identical to mine," I volunteered.

"All of the first-class compartments are identical on the Arkham Express, Detective. I take it that you are not an experienced traveler of the rails?"

"I don't get around much."

The warmth had left his demeanor, and he reached into the breast pocket of a Glasgow brown tweed. I instinctively started to reach for my gat but stopped when he produced a tan leather pouch. A weird figure embossed on the leather caught my eye:

a familiar one, the likes of a tentacled mollusk. The small leather bag next yielded a hand carved skull pipe. The detail and artwork were impressive. The jawbone of the skull acted as a stand when Nigel set it on the armrest and proceeded to fill its bowl. From the pouch, he stuffed the pipe with tobacco the color of olives. I watched with fascination as he struck a wood match on the bottom of his shoe and lit the pipe's contents. A thick leaden smoke curled around his features as he drew hard on the stem keeping the fire alive. He tossed the extinguished matchstick to the oriental rug. A musty herbal odor filled the carriage. "This is an exotic blend, Detective. If you care to try it, I have a spare pipe."

"No thanks, I like my tobacco a nice shade of brown." I removed a Lucky from the pack and lit it with my Zippo. I let it hang from the corner of my mouth. It was a counter-offensive against the strong odor given off by his pipe. "Your accent, sounds British?"

"No," Nigel answered with a sly grin. "I am from Ontario."

"Long way from home?" I sort of asked taking a drag on the Lucky.

"I am taking in the sights of your lovely countryside."

"Arkham ain't that lovely, pal."

"My scheduled stop is Providence, although your Arkham sounds intriguing. I've heard a few interesting things whispered about it. I am a writer, Detective. Your City's reputation could be inspiring. You see I write to please myself, in defiance of contemporary taste. I like to think my works would have delighted Poe; possibly Hawthorne, or maybe even Lovecraft. They are studies of abnormal men, abnormal beasts, abnormal plants. I write of remote realms of imagination and horror, and the colors, sounds, and odors which evoke emotional discomfort in my readers. You might have read some of my works in 'Weird Tales?'"

"Can't say that I have." I was familiar with the magazine. My partner, Matthew Bell, read a lot of that stuff. At times his desk would be littered with dog-eared copies of "Amazing Stories, Black Mask" and the aforementioned pulp.

"I am a true epicure of the terrible, Detective," he professed holding in a lungful of smoke, then expelling it with a long savory flare. "I am a person to whom the thrill of unutterable ghastliness is the justification for my existence. That is why your Arkham may have an appeal to me. Tell me, are there lonely farmhouses in the backwoods; dark elements of solitude, grotesqueness, and ignorance that combine to form the perfection of the hideous?"

"You described it to the T. Can we dispense with the travelogue for a moment and tell me why we are not talking about the recent murder?"

"Oh, I'm afraid I won't be able to shed much light on the murder per se, but I did find part of the young lady's testimony in the lounge car inconsistent."

"How's that?"

"She said that she never left her seat since the Arkham Express left the station?"

"That's correct. What of it?"

"She did get up, Detective and leave by the back of the coach."

"Where did she go?" I stood up quickly anticipating a lead that I could follow up.

"Oh, I do not know. She was gone for only a few minutes. Possibly she went to the lady's washroom."

***

Nigel Guest was a guy headed for a padded cell. He took forever to get to the point digressing later from the matter of the moment going on and on about pale gray shores beyond time and space and other such nonsense. When he declared, "the tree, the snake, and the apple are the vague symbols of a most awful mystery! Seeds of a deed that move through angles in dim recesses." I made my way to the door. Nigel's eyes glassed over, and he shouted, "they are hungry and thirsty!" That was when I left the compartment.

Nigel may be a writer of sorts and nutty as a fruitcake, but if there was a kernel of truth in his account of the lady in blue leaving the Pullman Car to powder her nose it was time that I gave her the third degree. Get out the rubber hose Detective, I told myself. Oh, hell it ain't kosher to hit a lady, but in her case, I'd sure like to make an exception. And if what he said was accurate there was one more thing that marred Lady Blue's credibility. My wife, Nora, is a fan of Emily Brontë. From time to time she'll read me some of her poetry. You see Brontë was a poetess and only wrote one novel in her lifetime. So, when the dame said, "I've read all of her novels," it was a bald-faced lie!

Lady Blue became my number one suspect, but old Nigel was a close second. Anybody that nutty deserved scrutiny.

I leaned headlong on my tiptoes in the hall outside Nigel Guest's compartment being accelerated slightly forward by the braking train. The brakes hissed and screeched when the train slowed to a stop. Through the windows, depot lights haloed in the mist. The snowy station platform teemed with activity; a porter wheels a trolley, a woman in a suit and hat holds a girl's hand, who holds her doll, while standing beneath a sign that read, "Pennsylvania Station." The cook, Sarah Walker, hurriedly left a forward car leaning against the cold in a heavy wool coat. Several more passengers were leaving the Express and only a few, in comparison, got on board. I hoped that none of the departing ones was my murder suspect. Nine o'clock in the evening is an awkward time to board a train. Dawn wouldn't be for another ten hours.

I watched as a group of laborers slid opened a large steel loading door to a boxcar and loaded pallets of shingles inside. We were positioned by a water tower. The layover was also a stop to replenish water. The boilerman swung out the long spigot arm over the tender and "jerked" the chain to begin filling the boiler. For burgs too insignificant to have a regular train station, ones we were destined to stop at every fifteen miles, gave rise to the slang term "Jerkwater town." A man in a black bowler and a gray topcoat, a safe distance from the splashing water, stood talking with the train's engineer and a uniformed conductor. After a while, he walked away, and from my angle, I was unable to see if he got on board.

The train, with a terrific jerk, moved slowly forward. The Arkham Express forged ahead with a rumbling clatter as it left the station. It made a steadily increasing chugging sound. The whistle wailed like a forlorn call in the night.

***

I went back to the Pullman Car. Lady Blue was not there, but the guy with the hipflask was still seated where I last left him. I decided to take a different approach to question him. "Hiya pal, mind if I pull up a chair?"

"Be my guest," he shivered back.

It wasn't cold in there. It was hot and stuffy in the overheated car.

"Earlier I couldn't help but notice that silver flask of booze you keep in your back pocket."

"I know you are a policeman. Are you going to arrest me?"

"Nah! I leave that up to the Feds. Never been a fan of the temperance law. I wanted to drink to your health."

Some of the shivers left him, and he smiled. "Absolutely!" he exclaimed, a little too friendly for my taste, but a shot of decent whiskey right then would do me a world of good. I smiled back.

It was a classy flask for two he presented. I had only seen one like it once before. He yanked off a cap that became shot glass number one and then unscrewed the top that had been concealed underneath and voila the second jigger. His right hand shook while he poured. My stomach churned for a second time that evening. He had six fingers on his hand or more accurate an extra thumb. A sixth digit as a rare and separate abnormality was enough in itself to ponder, but what made it additionally weird was that the Lobo I extradited to the Big Apple, also displayed the same affliction. I tried to maintain my composure, but I don't think I did a good job of it. "Salute!" I braved and downed the amber liquid in one gulp. It had a different flavor than the cheap stuff I normally drink. "What kind of whiskey is this?"

"It's brandy, Officer, Courvoisier."

"Different, but tasty, thank you. What's your name, my friend?"

"James Fraley, Officer."

"He was awfully damn polite. After the verbal abuse I suffered from Lady Blue, it was a welcome relief. "You know that there was a murder committed on the train this evening?"

"Yes, I've heard."

"Did you observe anyone enter this car during that time?"

"No." he answered resuming his shaking.

"I don't see how that's possible, James. I have it on authority that the murder suspect hightailed it through here." I lied. "And from where I sit you had a clear view of that door," I jerked a thumb toward the connecting door to the dining car.

"I'm sorry, but I wasn't paying attention. You see I was playing solitaire most of the evening and I was caught up concentrating on the game.

On the little table next to where he sat was a pack of playing cards. The cellophane seal had not been broken. He lied. So far, nobody was giving me any straight answers. It was either obfuscation from the lady in blue or mystification from nut job Nigel, and then there was this guy. I was about to press James Fraley further when she strolled in; Lady Blue. I seriously considered asking James for another belt but thought better of it realizing that too much liquor on an empty gut would make me the dumbest man in the room. "Stick around; we'll talk later pal," I directed and left my chair.

"Hello, sweetheart," I said with a forced grin approaching my suspect number one, anticipating another brawl. This time I wasn't going to pussyfoot around. She lied to me twice; first about not leaving the Pullman and second about that Emily Brontë thing. She started to open her yap when the sound of the train's wheels contacting the rails increased in volume interrupting her. A breeze blew in. The door to the dining car connecting platform opened and bowler and topcoat entered.

He was a stocky fella, broad-shouldered with a pot on him signifying too much food and too much libation in his fifty-some years. "I'll be asking the questions from now on," he declared.

***

"Finding a corpse is a crime?" I complained. We sat in the abandoned dining car. He wanted to question me in private.

"In my jurisdiction it is."

"And just what is your jurisdiction, pal?"

"Pennsylvania." Bowler hat said exhibiting a cool manner.

"The entire state?" I challenged hoping to get his goat.

"Hardly," he answered appearing bored. "Pennsylvania Station Police," he added flaunting the badge he kept inside his hat exposing a bald noggin.

"A railroad detective," I almost laughed out loud. Then thinking better of it I handed him the notes I took from questioning suspects. The sooner I dump this on someone else's lap, the better. Then I could get on with my vacation. It was my turn to flash my badge. "Arkham Constabulary. I'm returning to my jurisdiction after extraditing a prisoner to the Big Apple."

He took the notes and then he said the bad thing. "I will also need your badge and your gun."

"Do you want your friends to call you lefty? Providing you have any friends." I don't think the railroad dick was used to people addressing him in that manner. He started to reach inside his coat. "Don't go for it, Mr. Railroad. You don't stand a chance." He was obviously startled. The not so tough guy, Pennsylvania Station Railroad Detective, unbuttoned his coat, opened it wide and displayed three cigars protruding from a breast pocket. They were cheap cigars. The nickel ones you get in a drug store. "Look, Detective, let's you and I start from scratch and play nice, nice. I promise not to shoot you if you promise not to shoot me," I smiled. I'd been doing that a lot lately. It did the trick, and he tendered me one of his five-cent stogies.

"A peace offering," he said a bit sheepishly. I guessed that he decided that he had been coming on too strong. Maybe he was having a lousy day as well.

I took the cigar, bit off the end, and lit it. It tasted like crap; I didn't say so; it was best not to offend. He leaned forward, and I ignited his with my zippo. "The return trip was going to be a vacation for me, but if you want, we can pool our resources and try to crack this case."

"I'll consider it. You are still a suspect. You were the first one to discover the body."

"Third." He looked confused. "The two lady cooks were first."

He wrote it down on the pad of paper I gave him. "I, of course, will have to question them."

"You're a day late and a dollar short, pal. I saw one of them leave the train at your Pennsylvania Station and I wouldn't be surprised if the other vamoosed as well. There's always the busboy. He came into the kitchen after I did."

I was about to give him Alvin's name when we were greeted by the uniformed conductor. "Ticket please?" he mechanically asked.

I handed him mine, and Railroad Detective just nodded in his direction. "Took you a good long time to check for tickets?" I contested.

"It has been a hectic schedule, sir," he answered marking my admission receipt with a ticket punch.

The train's brakes hissed and screeched slowing us to a stop. I looked at my watch. "We haven't been out of the station very long. It is not a scheduled stop."

"Maybe there's a cow on the tracks," Mr. Railroad speculated.

I noticed something peculiar. The conductor and Railroad made eye contact and exchanged guarded peeps. There was something fishy afoot. I got up from my chair and looked outside. It was about half-past ten when the train came to a halt. Heads poked out of windows. A little knot of men was clustered by the side of the line looking and pointing toward the front of the engine. Ice stalactites hung off the window sills. "Looks like your people are going to need you, Detective," I said turning from the window. My second-best friend had buttoned up his topcoat and was heading out of the dining car.

"I'll get my hat and coat and be with you in a minute," I called out as the door to the connecting platform closed.

***

I retrieved my trench coat from my compartment and stepped off the platform. The ground was slippery. The train's engineer, the conductor, and the railroad detective were huddled in conversation, steamy breaths in the cold night air. I was unable to hear what they were saying as I approached. Railroad Detective gestured frantically appearing to issue orders to the other two. "What's happened?" I asked.

"Ice, sir," answered the engineer turning in my direction with a lantern in one hand and an oilcan in the other. "Purely precautionary, sir. There is a switch up ahead, and I've sent our boilerman to inspect it. The station house between here and our next watering stop was shut down due to layoffs — no one around to daily examine the tracks, sir. We have orders to do the inspections ourselves when faced with adverse weather conditions. Last year a Baltimore & Ohio train encountered a frozen switch. The pony truck on the locomotive derailed, turning the engine and tender over. Thirteen people were killed. It is purely precautionary, sir."

FDR's "New Deal" sought to stabilize the economy but

unemployment stood at twelve million. While politicians proclaimed that the national economy was in good condition the railroad industry was in a state of deep pessimism. Capital investments were cut, and maintenance was deferred to the greatest extent possible. It made everything the engineer claimed seem straightforward enough. However, he also sounded rehearsed.

"We are just waiting for the boilerman's return and after a few maintenance checks," holding up his oilcan, "we'll be on our way."

Puffs of steam emanated from beneath the locomotive melting some of the ice and snow surrounding it. The blood curdling screams of many suddenly overpowered the sounds of the hissing vapor and dripping condensation that augmented the engineer's performance. Not again, I imagined. I tossed the five-cent cigar and watched it dissolve a hole in the snow. Then I hightailed it inside.

***

He was face down on the Pullman Car's carpet. Blood splatters haloed his head. It was Six-Finger Fraley. The right side of his skull was bashed in, and on the left was a small hole, identical to the one I observed in Donald Wheatcroft's noodle. And like Wheatcroft's, it was not made by a bullet, if it was, it should have partially closed. Did it go right into the brain? "There is no clotted blood at all," I said out loud to no one.

"Jesus!" proclaimed the Pennsylvania Station Policeman coming up from behind. "How on Earth did this happen?"

"Your guess is as good as mine; just got here."

"Is he dead?" He choked out. He looked like he was desperate to turn and run.

"As a doornail." It was obvious that Mr. Railroad Detective didn't have much experience in these matters.

***

James Fraley kept Donald Wheatcroft company in the refrigerator car. The two porters that stitched up Wheatcroft's remains in the mail sack had skedaddled at the Pennsylvania Station train stop. I guess they no longer had the stomach for train travel. The distasteful task was left up to the kid and me. Alvin Nash held the stiff's feet up while I slipped the mailbag over. The load was too heavy for the kid and me to carry the distance of six car lengths. So, I had to enlist the unwilling, but eventually yielding aid of Mr. Railroad. I thought the guy would lose his supper.

Railroad headed for the john when done, and I returned to the scene of the crime. Again, no witnesses. Only the few that stumbled upon Fraley's remains and they were useless. Lady Blue was nowhere to be found.

On the floor of the Pullman was the murder weapon. There were a few writing tables in the lounge car like the ones where James Fraley pretended to play cards. Copper clad eight-inch long paperweights the shape of an oil tanker car with the words "Hickok Producing Co. Toledo Oh." stamped into them rested on most of the tabletops. When the summer heat prompted passengers to open windows and fans stirred the air, paperweights such as these were both functional and a reminder that the business of America was business. The one I discovered had done its business effectively. Blood and hair adhered to a corner of the heavy paperweight. There was something sticky on the underside. It felt like jelly. I squeezed it, and moisture ran down my wrist. I turned the paperweight over. It was more of that damn bluish pus.

The hole in the head still mystified me. Both corpses had the same hole. If made by a small caliber bullet, it must have been of extremely low velocity not to exit either skull. And if you shot the guy why club him as well? Plus, in both cases, no one heard a gunshot.

***

We were lunching in the dining car. Nigel and me. I crossed Nigel Guest off my suspect list after the murder of James Fraley. He had two solid alibis. The conductor and Alvin Nash. The three of them had been playing Mahjong in Nigel's compartment when the murder was committed. It quickly became known that Alvin was a wiz at the game and taught his two playmates a three-player variation. The kid beat the pants off them. Unless they were all in cahoots, Nigel was off the hook.

The Luncheonette was extremely limited. The kitchen, of course, remained closed and while we were at the Pennsylvania Station stop the conductor bankrolled Alvin to commandeer some box lunches at the trackside café. Mine was a cheese sandwich and an apple. The bread was stale. Nigel had chosen the pressed chicken. After one bite he set the sandwich aside with disgust and concentrated on his apple. Probably wished he opted for cheese.

"All around us," observed Nigel between small dainty bites of his apple, "are people, of all classes, nationalities, and ages. They are strangers to one another, brought together as travelers. They sleep and eat under the same roof on wheels. Now, because of this unscheduled stop, they cannot get away from each other. We are all trapped with a deranged fiend on board.

It would make an interesting story for me to write if I wasn't scared out of my wits."

"Perhaps, it is not as random as you presume," I countered. "Maybe some or all of them are linked together in a conspiracy. It would explain why no one seems to see or know anything."

Nigel took another nibble of his sandwich as if his first assessment was a mistake. He smacked it down on its wax paper wrapper his features repeating the revulsion. "You are morbid, my friend. Maybe it's something you ate."

I almost laughed out loud. "You have to consider all possibilities in my business."

"You appear distant. It weighs heavily on your mind?'

"Too many variables."

"Which are?"

"Five questions," I announced, my right hand up four fingers and a thumb spread wide.

"Only five?"

"Yes, Nigel. Five big questions if answered would crack this case wide open. First, how did the murderer enter and leave the dining car galley without being noticed?"

"That is a tough one. Perhaps your killer was truly unclothed. A clever possibility. Blood would quickly and easily be washed off so that a change of clothes, simply stashed ahead of time in the lavatory, once donned would allow him to blend in with the other passengers."

"Yet no one saw anyone enter the Pullman."

"Unless it was one of them or a disguise maybe. You told me that you have not ruled out the possibility that the killer could be a woman. Did you inspect the Ladies Washroom?"

"I did not. That is worth investigating."

"What is number two?"

"Why do the victims have a tiny hole in their left temple?"

DEATH ON THE ARKHAM EXPRESS

"A bullet hole?"

"Possible, but even a small caliber bullet with a low velocity should have exited the other side of the victim's skull. Or at least have exhibited some form of additional cranial damage. Only a full autopsy will give us answers. You don't happen to have a bone saw on you?"

"Heaven's no."

"Number three," holding up three digits. "Why did the murderer only remove Mr. Wheatcroft's head and not Fraley's?"

"That is a difficult one. If a single killer, you would think that he or she would establish an identical pattern."

"Exactly, you are getting good at this Nigel." My hand up again with four fingers showing. "If blue lady is our suspect, how come her dress isn't covered in blood?"

"That I believe brings us back to the possibility of a disguise and the prospect of the Ladies Lavatory used as a changing room."

"Very good, Nigel."

"Thank you. I must say that it is obvious that you and your Lady Blue were not hitting it off."

"Yeah, there's a rumor going around that she had a mother." His observation made me stop and think. I thoughtfully offered, "And why does the color of that pus residue left at the scene of each crime seem so damn familiar to me?"

"That is your fifth question?"

"Yes."

"That has me stumped, and I am afraid that you are the only one that can answer it."

"I'll give it some more thought."

"You left out the six-fingered man," he threw down.

"He's just a loose end."

***

Nigel "the nut" made a halfway decent sounding board. I needed a willing ear to bend to my notions. My options were limited like the train. Most were hiding in their compartments or running away from me when I attempted to question them. It was while we were kicking around some of the ideas when a parade of railroad employees approached us.

The engineer, void of his lantern and oilcan, the conductor consulting his pocket watch as he moved, accompanied by the Pennsylvania Station Dick marched up to our table. "The boilerman has not returned," announced the sullen police Dick.

"I wondered why this was taking so long," I probed. "Have you tried looking for him?"

"A thick snow is falling," answered the train's engineer. "You can barely see your hand in front of your face."

"You got a light on the front of this buggy?" I asked. "And a few more lanterns?"

He nodded, "yes."

"Then let's put this train in gear. Drive slow while some of us will hang off the sides of the engine with lanterns in hand and you'll light the way ahead. And hopefully, we'll be able to spot him."

"But he was my fireman," the engineer protested. "I need someone to stoke the firebox while I operate the engine."

"I can do it!" announced Alvin entering from the Pullman end of the car.

"It's hard physical labor shoveling coal, young man," disputed the station detective.

"I was baling hay on my father's farm when I was six before the banks repossessed it," he shot back, chest pumped with pride.

"Then it's settled," I declared. "Time is wasting."

***

I held onto the left side of the engine's cab with my right hand and a lantern in the other sweeping to and fro as we crept along. Railroad cop did like me, hanging onto the right side of the cab. My khaki trench coat wasn't adequate protection from the cold. Icy wind penetrated my garb chilling me to the bone. In contrast, Alvin was sweating profusely shoveling black rocks of coal into the furnace. Visibility was extremely poor. In a short while, the engineer brought the locomotive to a slow grinding halt. "There's the switch he went to inspect," he shouted over the noise of the engine.

I jumped down, and my counterpart did the same. The falling snow had almost obliterated any evidence of the boilerman's existence. I could barely make out the faint impressions left by his boots. A deeper, but larger man-sized imprint visible next to the rail switch was rapidly filling up with snow. The railroad detective kicked some of the snow away from the depression. Beneath, it was stained with rusty patches; blood.

***

There was something else I noticed out there, in the cold. There was no ice on the railroad switch. Not a lick. I brushed a layer of powdery snow off the mechanism, and there wasn't even a trace of frost. Unquestionably, icicles were hanging off some of the cars closest to the engine. However, that was due to condensation from the steam train's boiler collecting on the windowsills put there by the forward movement. When surface temperatures are below freezing, you get powder; powdery snow contains less water. The switch had been dry as a bone. I didn't mention it to the railroad employees. Their actions had become suspicious to me. I was playing my cards close to my chest. I doubted I could get the Pennsylvania Railroad Dick to fess up if there was anything to tell, so I decided that when the opportunity presented itself, I'd question the other two. The conductor was the obvious choice, when we returned to the dining car, since the engineer was not within arm's reach piloting the train.

"I've got a curious impression, Mister Conductor."

"Of what nature, sir," he answered. He was white as chalk.

"What do I call you besides, Conductor?"

"Passworthy, sir. Denton Passworthy."

"Fancy name, Passworthy, but not as fancy as the game that you and your pals are playing."

"I don't know what you mean, officer."

I was gettin' respect all of a sudden. I guessed he recognized my cop sense. "This unscheduled stop. It's got nothin' to do with ice on the switch. What did you and Mister Engineer and the lousy Rail Dick cook up?"

"It was an unscheduled rail stop. Purely precautionary, sir."

"You mugs recite from the same script. Stop pussy-footin' around Passworthy, or I'll have you locked up at the next stop as an accessory to manslaughter."

He sputtered a few syllables, shook like a leaf, and chewed on his lip. "Manslaughter?"

"That's right, pal. Your boilerman has gone missing, probably dead. It's as cold as an Eskimo's hind end out there, and the guy is probably frozen stiff by now. Fess up, Passworthy. What's the real reason for this 'unscheduled stop?'"

"Honest, Officer, it was not my idea. I was only following orders."

"From who? The Engineer?"

"No, sir." He stopped chewing on his lip and started to chew on his next words, then abruptly became silent.

I unholstered my .45, produced a pair of handcuffs, and laid them both on the table in front of him. Like the flatfoot on rails, I chose the seclusion of the empty dining car to do my interrogation. He stared at my hardware and swallowed hard.

"The detective, sir. He instructed the train's engineer and me to bring about the stoppage. The engineer and I are required to abide by all directives from Rowley Line Security. Neither of us was mixed up in his plans."

I had to give the mug credit. At least he wasn't chicken enough to take his buddy, the Engineer, down with him. "What was the plan, pal?"

"He told us that he wanted time to question all onboard about the murder."

"Before the next major stop, I presume, where he would be out of his jurisdiction?"

Passworthy slowly nodded the affirmative; his head kept kangarooing up and down owing to a sudden jerk of movement. A whistle blew, there was a long, melancholy cry from the engine.

***

We were underway again, and Lady Blue still had not turned up. I hoped that she had not taken an unscheduled stroll outdoors like the boilerman. Several of the passengers came out of hiding when the train started moving. Locomotion must have instilled well-being in some of the commuters. Out of sympathy for the kid and probably wanting to put distance between him and me, Conductor Passworthy volunteered to replace Alvin Nash shoveling coal.

"What can I do to help, your honor?" Alvin requested; his face as black as the anthracite he'd been shoveling.

"First off, go wash your face and second search every car for the lady in blue."

"Who?"

"Tall lady in a blue silk dress reading Emily Brontë. When you find her, report back to me."

"Aye, aye, sir."

He was gone in a flash. While he was tracking down Lady Blue, I was determined to locate the Rowley Line Company Dick and give him the once over. Out of habit, I checked to see if a .45 caliber slug was chambered in my 1911 Colt. There was; I forgot for the moment, that I had cocked my weapon when charging into the dining car lavatory. Remembering the john, I also recalled my conversation with Nigel Guest. Check the ladies' room, dummy I told myself. The kid would probably not have the guts to look there. Well, on second thought, maybe he did have the gonads, then again, I'd better have a look-see before chasing after Rail Dick.

***

I don't make a habit of entering ladies' washrooms. This time I was going to make an exception. I was standing near the rear of the roped off dining car door summing up the courage to barge into the feminine boudoir next to it. I pushed the restroom door open ever so slightly, only a little more than a crack, with my shoe and politely enquired, "Hello, anybody in there?" No one replied. I raised my voice an octave or two and bellowed, "Anybody home?" Silence greeted me. I tipped toed in and cautiously looked about. The coast was clear. I let loose with a sigh and began inspecting the facilities. The first thing that came to mind was that the ladies' washroom was a lot cleaner than the men's. My wife would say that, "men can be such slobs." I had to smile. I guessed she was right although I'd never admit it to her.

There were more toilet stalls than in the john for men due to the absence of any urinals. Rather than kicking every single one in, as I had done before, I squatted down to peer beneath the doors to make sure that none were occupied. All were empty, and I examined each. The one farthest down revealed an interesting clue. It told me that Nigel's assumption was probably accurate. Someone, a quick-change artist, after washing the blood off, and in haste to dress and leave the premises left a tantalizing bit of evidence. A portion of a person's attire clung to the inside of the stall's door handle. A small torn fabric of blue silk.

***

I quietly exited the ladies' washrooms into the adjoining hallway in hopes of avoiding attention. A fist slammed into the left side of my skull. I was down for the count. It was the Dick! I decided right then that it would be his name from then on. Before I could get up, he was on me with a two-handed choke hold. I returned the punch landing a right cross alongside his puss. The black bowler went flying, and his bald noggin vibrated back and forth. I was losing oxygen fast. He stared at me with ghost eyes. There were no pupils. Solid white orbs with a devilish glare. I swung hard again, and his head vibrated mocking a tuning fork. His lips parted, and I was staring at a mouthful of yellow canine teeth. I started to lose consciousness when I heard a loud metallic, "clang." Dick became a sack of potatoes slumping to the carpet.

I pushed his comatose form off me and got to my feet. Chef Ann Hoade stood over the fallen Dick, a cast iron frying pan in hand. She looked a little timid, overwhelmed, and repulsed by the outcome. At that moment she was extremely charming to me.

"What the hell!" I choked.

Ann backed away from the fallen Dick and leaned against the hallway wall. "At the risk of sounding ungrateful, what the hell were you doing here?" I asked continuing to catch my breath. "I thought you left the train along with Sarah Walker."

"I came back to get my frypan," never taking her eyes off the man on the floor.

I removed my fedora, straightened out the crease in the crown, and plopped it back on. "You crossed over into a crime scene to get a pan?"

"It was my grandmother's. It was well seasoned for frying chicken."

"A family heirloom, huh?" I had to smile.

"Yes. I didn't disturb anything. I was careful to step around the . . . evidence. I put your rope and sign back in place when I left." She maintained her downward stare and sighed convulsively, "I guess I kind of hit him pretty hard."

"Hard enough," I answered, feeling for a pulse on his neck. "He's out for good."

The pallor left Ann's cheeks, and she appeared light-headed. I took her by the arm and escorted her toward the Pullman Car. She motioned for me to stop when on the connecting platform and gulped deep breaths of the cold outside air. Her heavy exhales hushed the "tchjk tchjk" of the train's wheels bouncing along the rails. Chef Ann regained her composure and announced, "I'll find Alvin and send him to you."

It went without saying why she was going to send the kid my way. We had another body to move. I watched her enter the Pullman and returned to the fallen Dick.

I was examining more corpses in one day than I would in a month of Sundays back in Arkham. It was becoming routine on the Arkham Express. The life had gone out of the Pennsylvania Railroad Cop when Chef Ann beaned him, so you can imagine my surprise when I detected movement about the Dick's head. The left side of his skull began to pulsate when I bent over for a closer look. As before there was no pulse, but something inside that cranium was laboring to get out, and my cop sense told me it wasn't a blessed event. A tiny piece of flesh, hair, and bone discharged onto the carpet. I recoiled startled and landed on my butt. A pencil sized hole materialized in his skull. I couldn't take my eyes off it. A white finger, more like a worm, squirmed halfway through the opening, wiggled around as if sampling the air, and then turning in my direction slipped back inside. Had it seen me? Did I frighten it back into its hole? I wasn't going to wait around and find out. I ejected a .45 caliber round from my colt and did the next revolting thing. With thumb and forefinger, I wedged the oversized bullet into the orifice, widening the opening plugging it up.

***

It was a struggle for Alvin Nash and me to get the remains of the Rowley Line Security Dick to cold storage. The guy easily topped two-hundred pounds. I placed his black bowler over the plugged-up hole in his head until we tied him up in a mailbag. It would be tough to explain to Alvin. Plus, I didn't want to scare him off. I was losing compatriots right and left, and I needed to keep him around. The kid came in handy. After that white worm played peek-a-boo with me, it was imperative that an autopsy on one or all of the dead guys were essential. I mentioned as much to Alvin, leaving out the creepy worm stuff.

"There is a doctor on board, your Honor. He has a seat in the day coach."

***

Doc Winfield was an old country doctor, a General Practitioner, with white hair and a bushy mustache to match. He was the type you could trust to give you two aspirins and call him in the morning. Winfield didn't practice surgery too much; occasionally a tonsillectomy, an appendectomy or two and the like. The Doc was traveling to Providence to visit his sister. He carried the obligatory black bag with the usual meds, tongue depressor, hypodermic, and scalpel. None of which was useful in hacking open a skull for a postmortem. Alvin Nash came through again. The kid rifled through the Engineer's toolbox and came up with a hacksaw. A fair substitute for a bone saw.

Doctor Winfield took some convincing but after plying the kind old gentleman with a series of pleas for his assistance he acquiesced. I bid him bring his overcoat and follow. It was colder in the reefer than outdoors.

Donald Wheatcroft, the dining steward's decapitated head, seemed the likely subject, to begin the autopsy. When I untied the bag holding his remains the old doctor did a step back and muttered a few biblical verses.

"That wound in his head, Doctor," I said. "It appears to be

made by a bullet, but as you can see, there is no exit wound."

Old Winfield frowned. "It puzzles me," he answered. "Of course, it was made by a bullet, but the wound should have partially closed up. Also, if it went right into the brain and lodged there, the cranium should be swelled. The authorities should be notified."

"Right now, Doc, I'm the only law on this train until we reach Providence."

He paused, paced slowly back and forth, pulled on his mustache and added, "Curious, there is no clotted blood around the wound. Did you dress it before laying him to rest?"

"Nope, this is the state I found him in." I wasn't going to tell him about the white worm in Dick's head either, the same type of opening in the skull. Didn't want to scare the crap out of him just yet or have him think I was a raving lunatic.

"This is truly incredible." The Doc paced back and forth again. "Self-infliction is obviously out of the question."

"Goes without saying."

"We must operate here. Could you hold the lamp for me?"

I brought one of the engineer's kerosene lanterns with me. I cleared a spot off a case marked "Frozen Beets" and managed to place Wheatcroft's noodle on top without throwing up my cheese sandwich.

The doctor washed his hands with a preparation he took from his bag and proceeded to hacksaw Wheatcroft's forehead.

"Now then," said the doctor as I held the lamp. "You must hold this steady and move this poor unfortunate man's head as I direct."

I did as he said, but I did turn my head. When he stopped his sawing, I turned and looked. I trembled at what lay before me. I stood there and gazed into the brain that the doctor relentlessly laid bare. Even in the still fidget air of the car, there was a dreadful smell. It had the odor of freshly turned earth and death. As I stared, I had the impression that the doctor was on the verge of collapse. He made a groaning sound, and I was certain that he had made a horrible discovery.

"Lower the lamp," he instructed. His voice was harsh, and it came from far down in his throat.

I lowered the lamp. In my career on the force, I have witnessed many gruesome things. Even a dame's brain splattered on the concrete. Until that evening I thought I'd seen it all. My experience told me how brain matter should look. Doctor Winfield suddenly straightened up and looked wildly about him, "It is a burning shame!" he cried out. "It's evil that has no shape, formless, yet it does have shape."

Winfield seized his bag and crossed to the door. With white, shaking fingers he drew back the steel latch to the exit platform. For a moment his tall, lean figure was silhouetted against a door opening of swirling vapor, and then he was gone. He retreated to the open platform and out of sight.

I stared after him for a few seconds that seemed much longer. Below the sallow glare of my kerosene lantern was the opened skull of poor Wheatcroft. Things moved. Squirmy things. As I rotated the light for a better look, some vanished while new ones took shape restlessly twitching, glistening in the yellow light. Even under the buttery color, they stood out as stark white against the remains of the pallid brain matter. And there was very little left to call a brain. The ashen remains of gray cells devoured to the size of a peach. The wiggling things reminded me of bulky larva. Creepy-crawly maggots, white worms. In an instant I realized that the shape-changing waning worms were, in actuality, one wrapping itself around the soft nervous tissue. When I grasped the nature of the thing, it leaped from the skull and grasped me about the wrist. I believe it was aiming to latch onto my head as well. However, my instincts kicked in and I blocked it midair with my right arm. It was soft, and it felt like a wet rag. I had a tight grip on one end with my fist, and a mouth materialized wide open as if I was choking it. I smashed my fist down on the case of beets and picked up the doctor's discarded hacksaw. I swung continuously like a butcher chopping meat at the long entrails that slithered out from Wheatcroft's cranium. Once in a dozen or more pieces, it became limp, and I dropped the last portion of it clasped in my hand to the refrigerator floor. It had to be ten degrees below zero in the car but sweat ran down my temples.

***

I was back in the deserted dining car going through the personal effects I took off the stiffs. They'd been piling up. Wallets, railway passes, Fraley's hipflask, and a small caliber automatic, a woman's gun to be sure, I had to smile, because I removed it from the Dick's overcoat. I checked, and it was loaded. I stuck it in my sock. When home I decided to get an ankle holster for it. I used to carry a small .22 revolver as a backup to my Colt, but years ago I gave it to a Catholic priest that needed it more than me.

Going through James Fraley's stuff, I came across his driver's license. Now things were beginning to make sense. Well, a little bit. Fraley was an alias. According to the license, his name was Russell K. Woodruff. The same last name as the Lobo I escorted to the hoosegow in New York. They were around the same age, probably brothers. I guessed that six-fingers ran in the family. Why was he on the train for the return trip? Did he see his brother off, said "goodbye," and headed north? Or was

he following me? Was it a revenge thing? Could be but he'd
have to sneak up from behind to get me because he was small in
stature and didn't present much of a challenge. I tossed his
wallet on the pile with the others and decided that his fate
would probably remain a mystery.

Ann Hoade and Alvin Nash were winded when they ran into
the dining car. "There's been another murder, Detective!"
declared Ann, swallowing hard, leaning against one of the
tables. It was after midnight. Was I ever going to get time to
myself? Oh well, no rest for the wicked.

***

The two ran ahead, and I followed. Out to the dining car,
through the Pullman, and into the first-class hallway. Ann and
Alvin stopped dead in their tracks. Curled up in a fetal position
was the crumpled form of Doctor Winfield. His left ear had
been torn loose, and it looked like someone had bashed his skull
repeatedly against the steam radiator. Another purpose of the
train's boiler was to supply comfort by piping steam into the
compartments. In the case of the Doc, "comfort" became an
oxymoron. I got down on all fours and examined the corpse.
There was a considerable amount of blood on the right side of
his head and, naturally, a pencil size hole in the left side. It had
become a habit I wanted to distance myself from; a good
thousand miles would do. I ejected another round from my
Colt and plugged the hole in his noggin. If this keeps up, I
thought, I'm gonna run out of ammo.

"What are you doing?" protested Ann, revulsion in every
syllable.

I looked up at her from my crawl, "I'll explain later." I
hadn't won her over. Alvin eyeballed me with mistrust. "Trust

me; this is a needed procedure. I'm afraid there is a greater danger on this train beside these murders. Something, as of yet, I am unable to explain. At our next stop, we need to evacuate this caboose. In the meantime, both of you are going to have to trust me." They were as silent as the dead man on the floor. My explanation, or lack of one, seemed to do the trick. They both relaxed some and considering that they were standing over the battered corpse of a kindly old gentleman, was a feat unto itself.

From my position, regarding my two compatriots, I detected movement along the ceiling. The intricate scrollwork on the massively patterned crown molding slithered. In an instant I spied a meandering snake the color of coffee, it zipped hurriedly along the carvings and vanished. I tightly closed my eyes then quickly opened them. There was nothing more than the stilled ornamented relief of the various wildlife and icons. The left side of my noodle was bruised and swollen from the punch I received from Railroad Dick. My head was throbbing. Was I punch drunk? Maybe my bifocals distorted the view, a smudge on a lens?

"What's the matter, Detective?" asked Ann noticing my dismay.

"Nothing," I said rising to my feet. "Too much mayhem and confusion and not enough rest."

"Maybe you should get some sleep," she offered.

"Oh no," I answered. I removed my fedora, ruffled my hair, and put the hat back on. "I never sleep until all's well with the world. One thing is for certain. The evidence is piling up, and I'm pretty sure I know who is responsible for all this."

"Who?" asked kid busboy.

"Lady Blue."

"It can't be her," asserted Ann.

"That's right, your Honor."

"How do you know?"

"I found her like you asked," stated Alvin.

"She was in her compartment when the murder was committed," Chef Ann attested.

Alvin confirmed her statement with a nod. "Ann and I found her resting in her compartment right at the time old Doc Winfield cried out for help."

"You saw her for sure?"

"No question about it, Detective," Ann verified. "There was no mistaking her. She was asleep, her eyes were closed, but she was sitting on the sofa bench facing the opened door to her compartment."

"The door was opened?"

"Yeah," answered Alvin. "She probably forgot to lock it."

I was back to square one, and my head hurt worse than ever; another dead body and no suspects. This time the three of us bagged up the corpse and lugged it to the reefer. Once at the door to my newfound morgue I bid the other two to wait on the opened platform while I carried the sack with the frail remains of Doc Winfield inside. Wheatcroft's divided noodle still laid on the frozen beets and I didn't think it was fitting for them to lay eyes on their sliced and diced fellow worker.

Ann and Alvin were dutifully waiting on the open-air platform when I returned. The train went into a curve and slowed to a grating metallic halt. I craned my neck and peered around the cars. We were positioned by a water tower. We had stopped at one of the small solitary station houses. I watched as Conductor Passworthy climbed over the coal car. His meticulously cleaned and pressed blue uniform covered in coal dust. Passworthy swung the water tower spigot arm over the tender and began watering. "Time for our evacuation," I declared.

***

I looked on from one of the windows in the deserted dining car. The place where all this craziness first began. At least everyone would be safe now. The door to the small wood frame station house was opened, and from my vantage point, I observed the remaining passengers from the Arkham Express file inside. It was overcrowded, but most managed to gather around the pot belly stove. It wasn't The Plaza Hotel, but it would be warm and safe until the railroad provided additional transportation. I was reasonably certain that none of them was the culprit. I had spent a good deal of time questioning the few travelers left on the Express, and if my hunch was right, the perpetrator didn't stand around the cast iron stove.

Ann Hoade and Alvin Nash begged to stay on board with me, but I wouldn't hear of it. Against their protests I made them gather up their possessions and scram. Ann gave me a peck on the cheek along with a parting comment, "You take care Mister Detective."

Alvin was less schmaltzy, "See ya in the funny papers, copper."

I was alone except for the engineer and Passworthy, the conductor. Oh yeah, and there was Nigel too. No amount of persuasion on my part would motivate him to get off. I thought about forcing him at gunpoint but soon gave up on the idea after he beseeched me to let him stay saying that he needed to get to Providence as soon as possible. Something about a horror writer conference there.

As the train slowly pulled away, I realized that I hadn't seen Lady Blue amongst the people crowding into the station house.

***

It was after 2 am. I was gonna take a rest, with my eyes open. I was traversing the Pullman Car to First Class going to my compartment when I saw her. Lady Blue was sitting in the same spot when I first met her. She peered into the open pages of "Wuthering Heights" with eyes that observed something else.

Lady Blue didn't notice me. Having nothing better to do, I amused myself by studying her without appearing to do so. She was no sweet patootie. Not a nice clean Campfire Girl and if we were to talk once again, I wasn't sure how to handle her. Play to your strengths, I decided, that's what my old man always said. She gazed up at me and seconds past before she spoke. "Hello, Detective," she looked tired. I was dead tired too from chasing ghosts all night.

"Why didn't you get off with the rest of the passengers?"

"There is death out there. It is too cold for me."

"There is death everywhere you go, sister."

"I am taking the Express to its final destination, Arkham. I have work to do."

"I didn't like her use of the words "final destination." When she uttered the phrase, it felt like someone walked on my grave. "A smart lady like you can get work anywhere. Arkham ain't a sweet place to get employment."

"If you haven't noticed there is a depression. On what corner do you want me to beat my tambourine?"

To use the obvious metaphor, she was a closed book. "Before, all I wanted to do was ask you some reasonable questions."

"To do with the matter in hand, the deaths on this train?"

"You bet. It was simple and straightforward. The

examination wouldn't have taken more than a couple of minutes."

"An excellent pretext, but a pretext all the same."

"For Pete's sake lady just answer me one question. Earlier this evening, did you notice anyone enter the Pullman from the dining car?"

"A few minutes ago, I did."

Evasive again, but I followed her lead. "Who?"

"That writer gentleman. He passed just here," she said at last pointing to the carpeted pathway between the Pullman seats. "I had a curious impression. It was as though a wild animal, a savage beast passed by me. And yet he looked altogether respectable. The body as a cage can be most respectable, but through the bars, the wild animal looks out."

"That sounds cracked, lady."

"It may be so, but I could not rid myself of the impression that evil had passed me by very close. I have merely outlined a poet's reactions."

A poetess. She'd been puttin' her peepers too long into Brontë's works. And I prevaricated too long; I cut to the chase. I removed the torn strip of blue silk found in the ladies' john from my coat pocket and dangled it in front of her nose. "Explain to me why I found this bit of your dress in the ladies' washroom?" I thought that would catch her off guard, make her slip up. No such luck. She didn't miss a beat.

"A woman does not discuss her toilet with a man, let alone a stranger. I am not in the habit of reviewing my private affairs with the police."

"When this iron horse gets to Providence the police maybe prying into your private affairs. The big house can be a lonely joint."

"I don't buy it, but your approach has softened since our last

45

conversation, Detective," she leveled a shrewd smile on me.

Again misdirection, she was a sly devil. "I get a little soft in the head every winter; it's the Christmas season."

"Merry Christmas you Lug." Lady Blue laughed. Her laughter slowed like a phonograph winding down. It was mirthless, and it gave me the shivers. Her eyes began to close, and I believe she fell asleep.

I looked down my nose at Lady Blue's dress, that book she'd been reading, and the strip of silk in my hand. The answer to my fifth question almost rocked me off my feet. They were all the same color and shade as the peculiar bluish pus that coated Wheatcroft's dead hands, the meat cleaver, and that copper paperweight.

***

I stretched out on the cushioned bench next to the window in my compartment. I just finished sharpening my knife, a stiletto, on a whetstone I kept in a carryon bag. I reviewed multiple times everything that the crazy dame in blue said to me while dragging the blade across the stone. Was Nigel the guy I was after all along or was she throwing me a red herring? When Fraley had his skull bashed in Nigel had a rock-solid alibi. I retracted the blade and slipped it into my shirt pocket.

I had drawn my .45 and laid it on my lap, my hand on top of the gun, and my finger on the trigger. I needed to rest, but sleep was out of the question until I reached home. I figured if anybody came in and saw me there accidentally catching a few winks they'd think twice about disturbing my beauty rest.

There was a knock. "Come in," I said. I lifted my .45 and pointed it at the door. It slowly slid to one side. Nigel Guest strode into the compartment. He seemed to bring a part of the night with him. He looked around briefly and plumped heavily down on the furthest sofa bench surveying me with frightened eyes. He removed a handkerchief from his jacket pocket and mopped his brow. It wasn't warm in my compartment, if anything it was a tad on the cool side.

"Pleased to see you," hopelessness oozed from Nigel's pores, then he plunged into a recital. "There is a form that is formless! It feeds."

I didn't know what he was smoking, but he was loopy, talking crazy like the lady in blue. "Hey pal, this is the third decade of the Twentieth Century not one of your cheap stories."

"I know that you think me insane," he said after a brief pause. "Did it ever occur to you, my friend, that force and matter are merely the barriers to perception levied by time and space?"

"Not since my first wife."

Nigel ignored my lame comment. He exhibited a painful expression pressing the hankie again against his forehead. "They slither down from the stars, through rotting black gulfs, and stalk us."

"Cut the crap; you're scaring me!" I kept my gun pointed in his direction. Any moment, I judged, he could fly off the handle and come for me. Nigel Guest was minus an athletic build, but after my run-in with the possessed Railroad Dick, I wasn't taking any chances. "Try to make some sense, Nigel."

The corners of his mouth curled into a smirk; the lips remained horizontal. "Lovecraft himself humorously referred to his mythos as 'Yog Sothothery.'" A dark expression replaced the halfhearted smile. "But there the comedy ends because I do not think that they are evil. Not in the sense that we comprehend evil. In their spheres, through which they move, there is no thought, no morals, no right or wrong as we understand it."

He was making my skin crawl. In his warped, twisted way was he attempting to reveal the murder culprit? "Okay, I'll play along. What are they?"

For a moment he seemed to recover his sanity. "A horror beyond anything your prosaic brain can conceive."

"Thank you," I said. Even with an eighth-grade education, I knew what "prosaic" meant.

"All human brains are prosaic," he explained. "I meant no offense."

"None taken."

Nigel's short-lived sanity slithered away. "What if, parallel to life we know, there is another life that does not die, which has the elements to destroy our lives? Perhaps another dimension, a different force that forages other lifeforms."

"I hope you're reviewing one of your plot synopses with me or I'm going to have to get you a straitjacket!"

"I hear them breathe." The train plunged into a tunnel. Outside the white snow beneath the dark early morning sky was abruptly engulfed in black. The engine's noise and the clickety-clackety along the rails amplified to a roar. Nigel's monotonous voice softly droned against the racket. ". . . devouring hopes, dreams, fears, secrets."

My ears were greeted by a moment of peaceful silence and a gentle metronome undercurrent of "tchjk, tchjk," when we exited the tunnel.

I turned from the view and observed Nigel crouching by the compartment's window staring at the opposite wall with feverish eyes. He suddenly screamed, "The thing wants room. My head cannot hold it. The pain is horrible!" He dropped the handkerchief and tightly clapped his hands against his head. "It is cold as ice. It makes a noise like a great big fly. It's sucking and sucking and sucking."

Nigel tumbled off the seat opposite me. I shouldered the .45 and rushed to his side.

He let loose with a soft whimper, "The earth will die screaming." With his last breath, his stare beheld something that wasn't there, "Beware of the Doels."

***

Without my aide-de-camp, Alvin Nash, I had no idea where the railroad stashed their mail sacks. I pulled the blanket off the upper bunk and wrapped Nigel's remains in it. I tied the bedspread corners tight around his body and proceeded to drag him out of my compartment.

There was something not right with the movement of the train. The night—the vast night started to brighten. We were slowing down. The flickering movement of a sign came into view through the many casements along the first-class passageway, "Providence." I watched the teeming activity of the station slip by through a windowpane. A handful of commuters on the boarding platform gaped and pointed at our passing. The Arkham Express slowed considerably, but we did not stop. We plowed on at a reduced rate maintaining our northeasterly route. The Providence Station should have been our next scheduled stop. Was the locomotive out of control?

Farther down the hall I noticed that the door to compartment number seven was wide open — the private compartment of Lady Blue. The light was on. I let the bundle I was lugging drop and headed for the open doorway. She sat there as pretty as you please. Only Lady Blue didn't move or flinch when I stood in the opening facing her. She was expressionless — the parody of a statue.

"We meet again," I gave her a lackadaisical salute.

"A terrible and unspeakable deed has been done," she spoke with the same husky tone, drawn-out and sluggish. There was something unusual about that voice. I got wind of the notion that it came from a different direction.

"Switching from poetry to prose, sister?"

"It wants to wallow in the night, to procreate."

It wasn't a fanciful notion. Lady Blue's voice lacked the common characteristic we all experience while conversing. My blood ran cold. When she talked, her lips didn't move. There was no facial expression at all when she spoke. I summoned up the inner cop and took a step into the compartment's interior. It demanded investigation. A little voice told me not to. Her head did not turn to follow my movement. Blue lady never altered her gaze from the opened doorway. I took another step toward her then halted. Ruffles in the blue silk dress parted on her left side. My throat went dry. I swallowed hard. I wasn't staring at a lady's underthings nor bare skin. There was a gap where undergarments or flesh should have been; a dark crevasse in her side that seeped blue bubbling jelly.

I stepped back, falsely reasoning for a split second that she needed medical attention. I gave up the brainchild the moment it entered my head. It became obvious right away that Lady Blue was not human. I wondered if she had ever been living at all. I detected movement out of the corner of my eye to the right. Instinctively I drew my weapon. It was that same brown crap that I believed I imagined slithering along the woodwork. It ran down the compartment's mahogany window casing and deposited on the purple cushioned seat. The damn thing had to be six-feet long!

There was a chambered round in the .45, and I had replaced

the two slugs employed to plug holes in the heads — eight in the clip and one in the chamber. Nine rounds I could let loose as fast as I could pull the trigger. I pointed the gun at the brown snake with a shaky hand.

The brown thing did not coil upon the purple sofa, rather it bent and formed to the bench like a child at play creating a seated human shape with a pipe cleaner in a toy car. But it wasn't a snake! A tube-shaped body segmented akin to a one-foot diameter godawful worm. The nightcrawler exhibited a belt-like glandular swelling of muscles that flexed, and a pair of arms outstretched. The puffiness ceased. There were arms with three-fingered hands, then the action repeated, and there were legs with oversized feet and enormous toes. Between the legs was an anal segment with bristle-like hairs.

If I shot the thing would the effect, I reasoned, be like using a pile of manure for target practice. I decided it was worth a try. I was attempting to take aim at the monstrosity, trying to decide which part might contain a vital organ, when the top outer layer of cylindrical muscle inflated into a bloated fleshy lobe. An eye formed with a toothless mouth below.

"Shooting me will accomplish nothing. My existence will soon expire," the words formed in a moist sloppy orifice. Was I off my noodle? One of us was, and it sure wasn't him, her, it, or whatever? I had to be hearing things. Because wrapped within those sloppy syllables was the voice of Lady Blue. Right then and there, between the smell of death and stumbling against corpses, I wished I had jumped from the train at that small station house along with the rest of the passengers. The hitch was in my giddy-up. I plopped my backside down on the bench opposite the talking nightcrawler. To say that I was at a loss for words is an understatement.

***

The clickety-clack along the rails sledgehammered my skull. The one big eye of the giant segmented earthworm stared at me. "There is a force that emits energy which passed from my world where it creates a new form of cell life."

I was powerless to speak, immobile, fixed to the bench where I sat.

"They have broken down all barriers."

Still glued to my seat I kept my gat pointed at the tube-shaped cowplop. Each segment enabled the worm to move. It expanded and contracted conducting respiration through pores in its dark brown skin. Night Crawler must have utilized a transport system composed of fluid, either that, or they didn't use toilets on his "world," because a wet spot expanded around it on the purple cushion. There was a smell; like freshly tilled soil and rotting leaves.

I decided to give the damned a chance. If I ever write my memoirs no one will believe that I talked to a worm. "There's a poor chap out there," I pointed vaguely toward the door and the bundled-up Nigel. "He was fighting off something—I don't know what. Little white worms in his skull?"

"Mind parasites," Night Crawler's voice still had that far away eerie element that was feminine.

"What is a Doel?" Normally I'm very direct when interrogating a suspect. Fire a loaded question smack dab between the perp's eyes. In Night Crawler's case, it was a lousy metaphor. However, it is also difficult to ascertain if I caught the big worm off guard, although he did answer the question directly.

"A terrestrial word of yours. Our race is the Megadrile. We have studied your kind from afar for a very long time and until now never interfered. We learned of the term from our observations. It comes from your ancient Greek language. No such life exists in your world, only viewed sometimes in the dreams of the very few, your highly sensitive artists and makers of stories. They move through geometric curves and angles."

"So, what are they?"

"Doels are tiny, flesh-devouring creatures who inhabit our plane of existence. On our world, their lifeforce is pure energy. Doels are invisibly shrouded in night and chaos. Unfortunately for your kind, once they cross over into your domain, the Doels' energy seeks to reside and feed in animal neural tissue, especially of the brain and spinal cord, that contains cell bodies as well as nerve fibers. They can animate a host when the need arises. Doels eat their way into corporeal form multiplying until the host ceases to be useful."

I thought that Nigel had scared the crap out of me with his morbid ramblings, but his prattle paled by comparison to our confab. Fear mixed with apprehension drove me to continue the dialogue. "My friend said that there is no thought, no morals, no right or wrong as we understand it."

"As you said," put in the Worm. "Only the desire to multiply. The Doel are without shape, they are formless until they feed . . ."

"How far can they reach?" I groaned.

"The distances of Earth to things that have traveled through space is minuscule. A mere trifle. They will overrun your planet. They will utterly destroy."

"And then what?" Although I didn't want to, it was a question that needed asking.

"The instant the Doel are Earthbound their limited awareness only knows three things; to eat, to grow, and procreate. When their food source dries up, when their numbers increase at a far greater rate than the cerebral cortex and cerebellum of all living creatures, they will atrophy, their existence will cease. Without biological life forms, only vegetation remains and without photosynthesis; the carbon dioxide-oxygen cycle, all plant life will wither and rot."

The thing's arms and three-fingered hands flared out as if expressing an emotion. "Their life and later their extinction will take away all from the Earth."

Revulsion overcame me. A sickening in my stomach of such magnitude never experienced before. Was everything I was learning from Night Crawler factual or a ruse? Was it an outer space red herring meant to mislead me? I did walk in on it exposing the true nature of Lady blue. Was there greater treachery? I had experienced, first hand, the many holes in the victims' craniums, and that disgusting white worm thing revealed by Doc Winfield's grotesque post mortem. It made what I heard credible. A horror without form that enters brains and clothes itself in human thought until the crawling, fleshless obscenity sucks the life out of its human host!

"Besides eating their way into existence, how did they get here in the first place?" I dared to ask.

"Harmonic resonance, it is a diverse and varied phenomenon seen in countless forms throughout the universe, from gravitational orbital resonances to electromagnetic oscillations, to acoustical vibrations in solids, liquids, and gases." Night Crawler's cylindrical torso swelled dramatically and then contracted. Was breathing difficult for it? "Harmonic resonance," it picked up again, "spans a vast range of spatial scales, from the tiniest wave-like vibrations of elemental particles, to even the subtle timbres of lifeforms. It is a power of attraction. In the case of planet Earth, there were two attracting elements."

I stared at the wormy thing waiting for "It" to continue.

"The wheels of your metallic conveyance contacting a rail generates sound waves which travel further than the rail and the air. It makes an ideal positioning signal for the Doel."

What, at times, I thought that the "tchjk tchjk tchjk" sound was soothing while at others an annoying pain in the head, became a homing pigeon for a thing from outer space. Amazed I asked the obvious, "You said there were two attracting elements. What's the second?"

"You, Earthly Detective."

I was dumbfounded. What the hell was Mr. Worm driving at? Me? Before I could sputter a few syllables "It" persisted with its tall tale.

"There is something about you that is different from other Earth dwellers of your kind. You vibrate contrary to the rest of your race."

Inside I was shaking like a leaf, but I knew that wasn't what the oddball creature meant. "This is crazy. I'm no different than any other guy on the street."

"It is there, I assure you. I can feel it also. Reach back into your mind Earthling. Something in your past may have altered your bio-harmonics."

There was nothin' special about me. I put my pants on one leg at a time and could drink booze with the best and the worst of them. What the hell; and then, a creepy feeling overcame me. I started to review my career on the force.

I work at Station House 13. I am the head of the Mythos Division for the Arkham Police. I investigate any and all things that go bump in the night while at the same time trying to discover their hole-and-corner intent. I hunt down things that can be misshapen, vague or unseen, and at other times, material horrors, all of which usually leave bloody trails wherever they go. I took out a band of ugly little Pilot Demons by burning my house down around them. Besides being homeless for a while, nothing special or singularly unusual happened. I blew the head off an Innsmouth bastard with my .45, but the fish face never touched me. Then it hit me like a ton of bricks. Could it have been Corvus Astaroth, the Night-Gaunt? When I impaled the S.O.B. with an iron sword, I got a tremendous electrical shock. Did that have a permanent effect on me?

"Realization presents itself on your features, Earthly Detective."

I didn't like being called "Earthly Detective," but I didn't say as much. Worm didn't have any features for me to read. I was listening to a bulbous head that resembled a pile of crap with an eye and a mouth.

"This is not my first-time journeying to your world."

"So, your kind are infiltrating our planet?" I threw down the gauntlet.

"The Megadrile are not invaders. I am a police-man. Before we could seal the hole in our plane of existence that allowed the Doel to escape, some came here at another time within your sphere. The woman that plummeted to her death in your place of residence . . ."

"Arkham?"

"Precisely, I hurled her out of the window. The Doel had infected her. The collision with the ... what is your word? 'pavement' destroyed the parasite and any chances of it multiplying."

"Yeah," I said disgusted, angry, and sickened. "I was there."

"Precisely again, you see now the attraction?"

"No!"

"Then there was the prisoner you were transporting."

"What about him."

"He never made it to confinement after you released him to the authorities. The Doel were growing inside him as well. When and if you return to your Arkham you may learn through your information services about the criminal with the missing head. They will never find it. I disposed of it along with the Doel that resided inside."

I didn't like it when the worm said, "if you return to your Arkham," but I chose to ignore it because it solved my chain of murders. I didn't have all the details yet, but that would probably come later. How do you collar a six-foot worm? Where do I clamp on the handcuffs? "That explains all of the killings on the Arkham Express doesn't it?"

"I am regretful to be the executioner, but it is true. The infection had to be eliminated. An observer on our world, for a period of surveillance, left a portal open too wide and too long outflowing the Doel to your side. The hole has since been sealed. As a regulator, I was able to pass over. My obligation is to police the dimensional barrier. Since the discharge, the task that laid before me was to eliminate all the Doels that crossed-over. I have done as such except for the ones occupying your metallic conveyance. Only I am unable to finish my assignment."

"Your assignment? What else is left to do? Everyone is dead on this train except for me. Hey, don't get any ideas, pal!"

"No Detective, you are free of the infection. I don't know why? Perhaps your bio- harmonics makes you immune, or maybe it is what you Earthlings call 'luck.' Your 'luck' was good as well when you put the bodies of the infected ones in the cold room on wheels. The reduced temperature slows their rate of reproduction. I was going to destroy the contents of each victims' skull, but there was always interference. Your conveyance on rails . . . "

"It's called a railroad train." His misuse of the term irritated me.

"Your 'train' is so crowded that it became an impediment to my intended destruction of the Doels. The one you called the 'boilerman' was simple to dispose of outdoors, cloaked in the nocturnal freezing rain. However, the passengers inside made my concealment practically impossible. Soon the seeds the Doel have planted will mature and escape their confines. Mankind will be overrun."

Somehow a written confession from a worm didn't seem plausible. "So, you bashed skulls and ripped the head off a poor soul to accomplish your 'assignment.' Wasn't there any means at your disposal besides killing them all?"

"They were mercy killings. Once infected by the Doel there is no turning back. The . . . decapitation . . . was my solitary combative confrontation." Night Crawler's inflating and deflating respiration increased. "I became skilled at other methods since. The conflict left my fluid mechanics ecosystem damaged. I can function outside of it for only short periods. The impairment also made me unable to return to my Megadrile World."

The blue pus and the meat cleaver all made sense to me. A fight probably ensued and the dining car steward, Donald Wheatcroft, must have got in a few licks with the knife before going down. Did the blue stuff drive the thing I came to know as the dame reading Wuthering Heights? I cocked my head toward the shell of Lady Blue, "This is a robot?"

"It is not self-propelled, merely an abstract, a transportation device, both terrestrial and celestial. It is a quantum prosthesis."

"You were inside operating IT?"

"Precisely."

DEATH ON THE ARKHAM EXPRESS

"Can't the quantum whatchamacallit be repaired?"

"That would be for the mechanists of my world. I am simply a police-man."

The big worm's ballooning increased. "You left out two others on the train."

"The pilot of this device on wheels and its helper?"

"Precisely." I relished the opportunity to pilfer his lingo. "The engineer and the conductor?"

"They were infected as well. I disposed of them into the boiler's firebox. My vital force is ebbing. I did it with all the strength left to me. Their bodies will serve as the last source of fuel for this conveyance. Soon it will slow to a stop. Eliminate the Doel before that happens. I can no longer apprehend the mind parasites. The quantum prosthesis is breaking down. It has never happened to our kind. The consequences of its deterioration have only been theorized. It may implode. It may create a cavity in the abyss. We, I am afraid, do not know. Move quickly; the Doel must be utterly destroyed."

"How?" my voice squeaked a bit.

"Incineration," the worm answered weakly.

"Burn all the bodies in the reefer!" I hollered.

Night Crawler inflated even more. Soon there would be little room left in the compartment. It outstretched a hand as if to say "Yes." I skirted around its ballooning form and headed for the exit. Halfway out of what was once Lady Blue's private compartment I heard an expulsion of air pronounce her last words, "Beware, Detective, in humans the cerebellum plays an important role in motor control."

When in the first-class passageway I heard a loud soggy "kerplop." I wasn't about to look back and find out what color now decorated the interior of compartment number seven.

The last words uttered by bogus Lady Blue stung me. I

looked to where I had dragged poor dead Nigel. The blanket I used to wrap up his corpse was still there. Nigel Guest wasn't in it.

***

Fire, fire, burn them up, cremate the remains of the victims was all I could think about as I ran out of first-class, through the Pullman and into the dining car. I had my Zippo, but that was pretty much useless without something to ignite. In the dining car, where I last interviewed Conductor Passworthy, was the kerosene lantern the engineer loaned me. It was a good size lamp for signaling with a half-gallon reservoir. It wouldn't be enough, I decided. The bodies had been piling up in the reefer, and I was going to need a greater amount of flammable substance.

I removed the rope and pasteboard sign across the entrance to the galley. I tossed them to the floor. There was no need any longer for a police barricade. The stains of slippery red blood on the galley deck had dried to a crackly chocolate shade when I stepped on it. I found what I needed in the icebox, a two-gallon bucket of lard. Lard is combustible like wood, it will burn if you get it hot enough, and the kerosene will be its fire starter.

I kept a watchful eye as I headed to the refrigerator car. Dead Nigel probably walked around, and I wasn't about to let him catch me off guard. At the open-air platform, I unlatched the door to the reefer. The racket made by the steam train was louder outside, the clickety-clackety sound of the wheels bouncing over the rails now took on an eerie quality. The noise was shrill.

With the door shut and the noise of the slowing train

muffled, I drew the bolt barring entrance from the outside. Nigel hadn't been close behind and this, I thought, would stop him from sneaking up on me. Once the bodies of the victims were cremated, I would hunt down Nigel Guest.

The task was gruesome, but according to Mr. Worm, necessary. I went about scooping handfuls of lard and smearing the stuff on all the corpses. The job of spreading the greasy mess over the stiffs was a stomach-turner. At least they were all clothed. Their attire would help to feed the flames. It was an ugly thing, but it had to be done. I poured a fair amount of the kerosene over of each. I was counting heads and the headless, wiping my hands on my handkerchief when I realized that Railroad Dick's body was not amongst the deceased. I looked up and expected him to be standing somewhere within the car's interior. I was startled when I saw Nigel grinning at me. His eyes were white without pupils, and like the Dick, his teeth looked more canine than human.

I unholstered my Colt, slipped the thumb safety off, aimed at his forehead, and pulled the trigger. The .45 caliber report was deafening echoing off the metal walls of the refrigerator car. The top of Nigel Guest's head blew off exposing a writhing mass of white finger worms. The massive wound didn't slow him down a bit. He looked like a bleached witch. Dead Nigel came for me arms outstretched. The oil lantern rested on the case of kumquats where I last left it. The filler cap was off. I scooped it up, poured the remainder of the kerosene over his noggin, and ducked in time to avoid a clobbering. The punch that missed threw him momentarily off balance, and I stepped to his left dropping the empty engineer's lamp. Nigel advanced with a victorious devilish grin. I flipped open the top of my zippo, spun the wheel against its flint, and ignited his opened skull. Nigel flailed about blindly, the top of his head a flaming torch. He swung to the right, arms still outstretched, then to the left; I was able to keep a safe distance.

I undid the locking bar to the side loading platform and rolled the huge door to one side. Nigel staggered close and fell to his knees. The opened crown of his blasted skull smoldered and turned a crispy brown. We had been traveling along the shoreward realms leading to Arkham. I planted my shoe in the square of Nigel's back and shoved. I watched his toasted form tumble over the rocky coast. Through the dense fog, I could barely make out his shadowy outline. Nigel bounced across massive boulders and, farther down, into the surf. The Arkham Express slowly moved along until I could no longer catch sight of him.

The lighter was still in my hand after Nigel departed. I lit each recumbent form igniting first the kerosene which in turn, as the heat increased, kindled the lard. The flames rose high, fire and ice. The mobile Viking funeral and my confrontation with Nigel caused me to be careless. The stocky baldheaded shape of Railroad Dick materialized before me. He must have been crouched down amongst the many crates waiting for his opportunity to pounce. The bastard sucker punched me again. It was a hard right. I didn't go down this time, but back peddled squarely into the steel frame of the large loading door. A stabbing pain shot up my spine. I drew my .45 only to have it knocked from my grasp by yet another blow from the Dick. I watched as my gun tumbled to the grass alongside the railroad tracks. He took the third swing, and I ducked this time. His fist struck the steel doorframe with a loud "clang." It didn't seem to faze him. The contact his fist made with the frame must have broken every bone in his hand, but he didn't flinch.

I countered the Railroad Dick's attack with a right cross followed by an uppercut. He stood his ground, smiled, and let me have it again. He landed a punch to my chest, and I almost lost my balance toppling backward toward the open edge of the traveling refrigerator car. The heels of my shoes hung precariously over the threshold. My arms swung wildly, out of control, and I caught hold of an iron ladder rung. It led to the roof of the reefer. I think that the Dick was surprised that I didn't fall out like Nigel, if the walking dead can ever harbor the emotion of astonishment. Dick just stood gawking at me. Maybe it was the movement of the fog-shrouded landscape sliding by that momentarily mesmerized him, or maybe he was truly amazed that I didn't take a backflip. Nevertheless, it gave me the few seconds needed to scale the ladder to the roof.

We were traveling below thirty miles per hour, and the train kept slowing. I remembered what the Night Crawler said, that all the Doel things must be "utterly destroyed" before the train came to rest. Right then I wasn't that concerned about the worm's warning. The wind was whipping topside, and I had to jamb my fedora tightly on to my noodle to keep it from blowing off. If my luck held out, maybe Railroad Dick will burn up with the rest of the cadavers below and I would ride out the ever-decreasing speed of the Arkham Express until it ceased moving. Luck was not on my side. I witnessed the bald pate of the Dick rise above the ladder. His head was just above the roofline, and before he could climb higher, I ran over and kicked him square between the eyes.

I stuck like glue. The Dick had grabbed my ankle, and I plummeted to my backside. I tried to kick loose from his iron grip, but he held me fast. I removed the stiletto from my shirt pocket, ejected the blade, and buried it to the hilt in the Dick's wrist. The long blade of my stiletto jutted out beneath the heel of his palm with the handle juxtaposed on the other side of his wrist. There was no blood. I don't know if it was the shock of being stabbed or that a crucial zombie muscle had been severed, all the same, he released his grip. The action gave me time to get to my feet. I swayed with the movement of the train. Zombie Railroad Dick climbed the last remaining rungs of the ladder and faced me once again.

My jaw, back, and chest throbbed from the pummeling I took. I was winded. I can stand toe to toe with the best of them, but fighting this guy was worse than going three rounds with the Manassa Mauler. The Dick advanced, and I stepped back being careful not to lose my footing. He was the most menacing opponent I had ever faced. The .45 caliber slug I had plugged up the hole in his head with earlier that evening, popped out and fell to the roof of the reefer. His white pupil-less eyeballs replicated the pale shade of the worm that slithered out of the cavity and draped over his cheekbone. Moonlight reflected off his shiny bare scalp. With disgust, I watched as more holes popped open and his head became a living Medusa of white worms. The grin never left his chops. The maniacal look on his puss and his wild swinging punches allowed me to get in a few of my own. The Dick telegraphed one, and I blocked with my left. I wasn't so fortunate with the next one. Unable to counter quickly he let me have it right on the button.

I was lying on the metal roof trying to recall why I was so cold. The walking corpse of the railroad detective stood triumphantly over me. Dazed, I watched as he leisurely withdrew my stiletto from his wrist. The bloodless blade gleamed in the fog-veiled moonlight. He raised the knife high. It would be all over for me in seconds. I reached for the small caliber automatic in my sock; the Dick's, once upon a time piece. I aimed upward and pulled the trigger. I kept pulling the trigger until, after five-rounds, the gun jammed. At least three of the slugs struck him in the face. There was a bullet hole in the left side of his forehead, and his right eye had been torn out hanging by a thread. I tossed the cheap gat aside and got back up. I detected another puncture wound above the jawline just as he toppled over. That took a while, I thought.

The fog was like a living thing. Its long fingers reached up and slapped relentlessly on my face, strengthened by the train's movement. It curled about the horizontal zombie railroad detective and me. The mist descended in great, grayish spirals on to our heads and from the Dick's long nose, moisture dripped. There was a grim look of determination in his one good eye; his jaw set firm. The three slugs I placed in his face had not done the trick. Three more white wormy things wriggled out of the bullet holes in his head. Beneath his dripping forehead, his eye became a thin slit as he struggled to his feet. The Dick slipped and fell on the slippery wet roof followed by another unsuccessful attempt. He seemed to be having trouble with his motor skills. It was probably that cerebellum thing.

Dimly ahead I saw the lights of a few lonely farms. There was a gap up front. I thought the fog was lifting or was it lifting? Several train cars forward hovered a hole, a big blue hole. The same damn shade of blue as that pus and the robot lady's dress. The Arkham Express slowly crawled into it.

A heavy force struck me crossways along the abdomen. It was a very long and large pipe. It knocked me off my feet and the wind out of my gut. I was swinging helplessly in space. I hung on for fear of falling. A water tower spigot arm had swung over the top of the moving train and caught me midsection. I kept swinging back and forth. The lengthy spigot pipe moved from side to side first colliding with the water tower, bouncing away to spin around and over the train cars only to turn back and repeat the process once it met the limit of its reach.

I caught a fleeting glimpse of Railroad Dick. The shot full of holes zombie with head Doels managed to get to his feet. He glanced at my swaying and then turned to stare at the blue gap in the fog. In the bat of an eye, the Arkham Express with the flaming refrigerator car and its living dead vanished into the deep blue void. The abrading clickety-clackety, clickety-clackety faded along with it — the harmonic response to the Night Crawler's dilemma of the deteriorating quantum whatchamacallit.

The spigot arm's swinging slackened, and I hung suspended over the railroad tracks. The subtle sounds of night greeted me. I could make out the faint wash of the waves against the rocky shoreline. It was when I was wondering if I would break a leg if I let go and dropped onto the wooden rail ties that I heard footsteps on the gravel beside the tracks.

"Hiya, your Honor," was the genial taunting voice of Alvin Nash. Alongside was Ann Hoade, still clutching her cast-iron frying pan.

I wanted to know how in heaven's name they got ahead of the Arkham Express, however, getting safely down was my number one priority. "Get me down from here!" I shouted.

Across the track, opposite the water tower, was an abandoned station house, another remnant of the Great Depression. Next to it was a weather-beaten ladder. Together Ann and Alvin struggled to drag the heavy wood extension ladder to my rescue. After leaning the spigot arm and the ladder against the water tower, I successfully made ground level. "Ok, I know that this sounds ungrateful, but how in the hell did you two get here in advance of the Express?"

"The signalman at Providence Station telephoned the manager of the station house we were at and said that the

Express was out of control and slowing down," answered Ann.

"Yeah, and we borrowed the station manager's car and raced ahead," Alvin piped up excitedly.

"I am embarrassed to admit it, Detective; we didn't get his permission to take his car. The law may end up on our tail. Alvin hotwired the ignition."

Alvin looked down at his shoes and place-kicked a pebble. How could I arrest let alone reprimand them for auto theft? I would have ended up in that big blue void along with all the dearly departed if it hadn't been for their intervention. "Forget about it," I said. "There are a lot of dead on the Arkham Express, and I am very glad that I am not one of them."

Less than a mile off I made out the neon lights of an ESSO Station. "Since you two have provided transportation, give me a lift to that gas station over there."

"What for?" queried Alvin.

"Need to make a phone call." I got in the backseat, Alvin sat shotgun and Ann drove. I delighted in the irony of a cop going for a ride in a stolen vehicle.

"Who ya gonna call, Detective," asked Alvin leaning over the front seat in my direction.

"Station House 13."

"You ain't gonna turn us in for stealin' the car are ya?"

"Not on your life. I'm gonna phone in my retirement."

ABOUT THE AUTHOR

Byron Craft started out writing screenplays, moved on to authoring articles for several magazines and finally evolved his writing style into exciting, sci-fi, fantasy, horror novels.

Craft has published three novels in a planned five-novel mythos series that reflects the influence of H.P Lovecraft. Byron Craft's first novel "The CRY of CTHULHU," initially released under the title "The Alchemist's Notebook," was the reincarnation and expansion of one of his most memorable screenplays. Craft demonstrates he is as capable a novelist as scriptwriter. Craft's second novel, "SHOGGOTH" continues with all the ingredients of a classic Lovecraft tale, with some imaginative additions. Followed by "SHOGGOTH 2: RISE OF THE ELDERS."

The first four books in the Arkham Detective series have been so popular that the enigmatic detective is back for another round. Craft enjoys this quirky character so plan to see even more of him in the future.

Craft enjoys writing full-length stories and would love to get feedback from his readers. Please visit his website: www.ByronCraftBooks.com

If you would like to read more books by Byron Craft, please visit his website: www.ByronCraftBooks.com or go to Amazon.com

The Mythos Project Series

The CRY of CTHULHU

This novelization of The Cry of Cthulhu film project is about a shell-shocked Vietnam vet, and his wife. They inherit an old country estate in Germany around the time his company transfers him to the same area. The two soon discover that the coincidence is really too good to be true.

Their home rests near a timeworn door into the earth that is poised to open, exposing all to a horde of four-dimensional beings. Soon the line between our reality and that other space-time will be blurred forever, leaving mankind to be consumed by shrill, shrieking terror. Only one man has the slimmest chance to save our planet and, even though he has no place to hide, he prefers to run. *[Book One]*

SHOGGOTH

An accepted theory exists that millions of years ago a celestial catastrophic occurrence wiped out every living thing on the planet. This theory may be flawed. Fast-forward to the 21st century. A handful of scientists, allied with the military, discover a massive network of tunnels beneath the Mojave Desert. Below, lies an ancient survivor, waiting...and it's hungry! *[Book Two]*

SHOGGOTH 2: RISE OF THE ELDERS

Who creates and controls the shoggoths? For Professor Thomas Ironwood and his heavily armed team, the answer is crucial. The fate of the free world hangs in the balance.

The solution? Return to the tunnels beneath the Mojave Desert, locate a gigantic subterranean vault and unlock the secrets it contains. Deadly primal secrets that lie in wait from a time before human life began!

Byron Craft once again takes us below the earth in this SHOGGOTH sequel enveloping us with tentacles, claws, and mucus glop. A talented fusion of Lovecraftian sci-fi, mystery, fantasy, and horror with a 21st-century twist. *[Book Three]*

The Arkham Detective Series

Cthulhu's Minions

A Novelette introducing the Arkham Detective. Cthulhu's Minions are Pilot Demons. Nasty pint-sized legless creatures that crawl on their hands with razor sharp claws and fangs. The diminutive beings must be stopped before they conduct one of Cthulhu's Old Ones to the back alleys and streets of Arkham, likewise the entire planet. The story takes place during the Great Depression, a spot in time where H. P. Lovecraft and Raymond Chandler could have collaborated. *[Book 1]*

The Innsmouth Look

The second story in the series that brings the detective back, investigating a murder and the kidnapping of a small child, which leads to Innsmouth by the sea, the frightful creatures that lurk there, and what they plan to call up from the depths. *[Book 2]*

The Devil Came to Arkham

Follow the Arkham Detective as he attempts to discover the source of a deadly epidemic. Is it the devil? Is it a Night Gaunt? Or Both? Find out when you read about a soul sucking creature that is bent on turning Arkham, Massachusetts into a ghost town. *[Book 3]*

The Dunwich Dungeon

In this final chapter, a seven-foot tall man in black has caused the Detective's good friend to go missing. A woman is brutally murdered in a museum, and mysterious artifacts lead us on a trail to inter-dimensional horrors. This time the Arkham Detective is armed to the teeth, and determined to avenge murder with mayhem. *[Book 4]*

Keep reading for an excerpt from Byron Craft's ***CTHULHU'S MINIONS***

BYRON CRAFT

72

CTHULHU'S MINIONS
By Byron Craft

Some say that they have always been there. A guy down on Delancey Street once said they were the remains of aborted fetuses. But the story I liked the best was told to me by an old tramp at the Nathaniel Derby Soup Kitchen. He said they were what was left over after a great war; a war that took place millions of years ago between good and evil. In my business evil prevails too often, but in his story, they lost. The Dark Ones, as he called them, were cast into some kind of underworld although a few managed to stay behind.

There were many stories, but I didn't believe any of them until Jefferson Buck had his face chewed off.

Jeff had been my partner back in the days when we wore the blues and drove black and whites. A few years later, a series of budget cuts put cops alone in their squad cars. A very dangerous situation for a policeman in a big city when there is no one to watch your back, a situation that followed us even after we both made detective. Oh sure, if we were investigating a homicide, the coroner would be at the crime scene along with a police photographer and one of the guys dusting for prints, or at the scene of a robbery there would normally be a uniform officer in attendance with me, but that was it. Most of the time, like all guys on the force, I was on my own, knocking on doors in some tenement or cold water flat questioning perps, looking for clues in back alleys and speakeasies.

Detective Jefferson Buck was found face down in the basement of the old Crowley Milner Building. The long forgotten department store had been closed for decades. Most of the windows in the twelve story brick structure had been broken out over the years, leaving it open to the wind. It had become a haven for drifters and street people. The guys from forensic said that Jeff had been dead for several hours before they got there. One of the bums, looking for a safe place to shoot up, found him. His screams carried through the opened windows and an officer on the beat heard the clamor.

Jeff's face was completely gone. I had seen something like this before. A couple of years ago I was called to the scene of an accident. A drunk had fallen off of a dumpster and cracked his skull for good. His face had been gnawed away by rats; not a pretty picture, but this was different. Jeff Buck's features hadn't been removed by a hundred little fangs like the drunk's; instead, it looked like it had been done by one size-able bite as if it had been made by a large animal.

"An alligator," a young forensic assistant blurted out. His assumption was quickly ruled out. There were rumors of alligators living in the sewers, but in all my years on the force, I had never seen one. Besides, there were several chilling things

74

in addition to Jeff's condition. His .38 had been discharged…six times. Whatever he ran into down there, he had emptied his Smith & Wesson into it before it took him down.

Also, there was plenty of blood at the scene, mostly Jeff's, but there was some that didn't appear to be his, next to an open storm drain. It was pale, very nearly pink, like veal, giving the impression of whoever this second party was; he must have been very anemic.

THE MYTHOS ALLIANCE

This is Byron Craft's tribute to a secret society of mythos authors and artists known only to a select few as THE MYTHOS ALLIANCE. Please check them out:

F. Paul Wilson . . . is an extremely prolific author, primarily in the science fiction and horror genres. He is the winner of multiple awards: two-time winner of the Prometheus Hall of Fame Award, 2005 World Horror Convention Grand Master Award, 2009 Bram Stoker Award for Lifetime Achievement, and twice has received the Prometheus Award for Best Novel. Mr. Wilson has requested that we showcase his most Lovecraftian tale, ***The Barrens & Others: Tales of Awe and Terror,*** available at Amazon

Sean Hoade . . . writer extraordinaire who, like a butterfly within a chrysalis, has masterfully developed inside a cocoon of literature and has, so far, written novels about a murderous RV salesman, Charles Darwin on the Beagle, and vis-à-vis Lovecraftian monsters attacking an Edwardian household. Mr. Hoade would like you to examine his novel **"Cthulhu Attacks! Book 1: The Fear."** Also **"Cthulhu Attacks! Book 2: The Faith"** co-authored with Byron Craft! Both available on Amazon.com

David Hambling . . . is an author that enjoys writing Lovecraftian weird science when he isn't working as a freelance technology journalist in South London. He writes for New Scientist magazine, Aviation Week, Popular Mechanics, WIRED, The Economist, The Guardian newspaper and others. His science background lends itself amazingly to his incomparable storytelling style. A favorite is his 1920's based science fiction novella series about an ex-boxer, *Harry Stubbs*, that blends weird science and Lovecraftian mysteries with a 21st century twist. Check out his works on Amazon.com!

C. T. Phipps . . . is a lifelong student of horror, science fiction, fantasy, and especially H.P. Lovecraft. C.T. unearthed a passion for tabletop gaming that compelled him to write and he eventually metamorphosed into a lifelong geek. Take a gander at one of his latest, *"Cthulhu Armageddon"* @ Amazon.com

David J. West . . . tells us, "I write because the voices in my head won't quiet until someone else can hear them." David writes dark fantasy and weird westerns. He is a great fan of sword & sorcery, ghosts and lost ruins, so of course, he lives in Utah with his wife and children. Peruse all his books @ www.KingDavidWest.com

Sarah T. Walker . . . is a writer and artist of dark subject matter, both fiction and non-fiction. Her art and writing have been published in multiple places from the Lovecraft eZine, to Audient Void, The Lovecraft Lunatic Asylum, and Shoggoth.net. You can learn more about Sarah on www.FictionFoundry.org

Eric Lofgren . . . is an awesome Lovecraftian artist. Eric is a recognized freelance illustrator in the RPG and CCG markets, a master at commercial illustration that includes collectible card art, book cover art and interior book illustrations. Please review his impressive works @ www.ericlofgren.net

Matthew Davenport . . . spends his time writing, reading, and working to promote and support writing communities in Iowa through his company Davenport Writes, LLC. Author of the Andrew Doran series, and over a dozen books, some Lovecraftian, he is an absolute MUST READ. You can keep track of Matthew on his Website: www.AuthorMatthewDavenport.wordpress.com

Paul Atreides . . . is an author, playwright, theater critic, and columnist. Troubled with abiding by those pesky rules of the afterlife, Paul has penned the ***Deadheads*** series as well as numerous short stories. To learn more about Paul Atreides go to www.paul-atreides.com

Kristopher Neal McClanahan . . . tells us that he is an artist, Con Man, soap boiler and teller of tales, currently living in Southeastern Idaho. You can see what he's made of by going to the Deeply Dapper website that features his artwork and links to his podcast and con appearances @ www.deeplydapper.com

Peoples Guide to the Cthulhu Mythos . . . is a podcast that follows the literary timeline of the Cthulhu Mythos from the big bang, to the cooling of our sun. Go there and listen to find what lurks in the darkness, and who created these lurkers. They also talk cult film, graphic novels, and contemporary mythos collections. Go, if you dare, and be scared @ www.pgttcm.com